ML

D1078517

7000399913794

MONTY McCORD

Monty McCord is a top ranch-hand with a hot temper. After killing young Hartley Billings he's on the run, and now old man Hunter Billings has sent his riders to catch up with him. But Ellen Watson and her Flying W crew are looking out for Monty — though putting him in charge of a herd is a risky move. Can he get two thousand cows from Colorado to Wyoming? Or will the lurking rustlers — not to mention Monty's pursuers — have their day?

CHUCK TYRELL

MONTY McCORD

Complete and Unabridged

LINFORD
Leicester

First published in Great Britain in 2013 by
Robert Hale Limited
London

First Linford Edition
published 2015
by arrangement with
Robert Hale Limited
London

A catalogue record for this book is available
from the British Library.

ISBN 978–1–4448–2395–0

Published by
F. A. Thorpe (Publishing)
Anstey, Leicestershire

Set by Words & Graphics Ltd.
Anstey, Leicestershire
Printed and bound in Great Britain by
T. J. International Ltd., Padstow, Cornwall

This book is printed on acid-free paper

To Monty and Ann McCord,
who so kindly allowed me to use
their names

1

Monty McCord topped the hogback above Mexican Hat and reined in his dappled sorrel. He threw a leg over the horn of his saddle and pulled makings from his shirt pocket. As he rolled the smoke his eyes scanned the village, then the approaches, then the heights of the mesas off toward Monument Valley. For a man with Hunter Billings's riders on his back trail, Monty made his smoke like he didn't have a care in the world. Hunter Billings. Gawdawful hunk of an old man who figured he owned Twin Forks Basin and the town of Watsonville, even though Frank Watson was there before him and even though Ellen Watson made it clear she wanted nothing of Billings's boy.

Women.

Monty figured Ellen was OK, as women went. She took over the Flying

W when old Frank passed on, and she did a rightful job of running the spread. Monty McCord admitted that. Ellen Watson was some woman. But she owned a ranch and Monty McCord was nothing more than a line rider. A good line rider, but not one who could sidle up to a ranching woman and make her notice. Besides, she was the boss.

Shit.

Dust showed on his back trail.

Monty snubbed out the smoke on his saddle horn, ripped the paper and scattered the tobacco. He rolled the paper into a tiny ball with thumb and forefinger and tossed it away, a habit born of years riding in the pine-tree country of Arizona's White Mountains. Suddenly he missed the peace and quiet of the Cooley ranch where he'd cut his teeth as a cowboy.

What the hell was he running for? He'd beat the shit out of nasty snot-nosed Hartley Billings. Tromped his ass. Then killed him.

Wouldn't have done that if the kid

hadn't shot at him when he was about to leave through the batwings of Woodrow's saloon. The kid's bullet had very nearly clipped Monty's ear, and worse, damn near holed his spanking new black Stetson.

Monty reacted. His hogleg was out and cocked as he turned. He touched off a shot as the pistol came in line and Hunter Billings's precious son lay dead.

Shit.

The cloud of dust seemed closer. A mile? Less?

Monty McCord was tired of the chase. Not because he'd ridden so far. Not because of the gaggle of hard riders on his trail. Just because of the unfairness of the whole thing.

Hartley Billings had pushed Monty. Pushed him hard, saying he was a two-bit puncher who'd die with a horn in his guts or pitched from his horse into some worthless bottomless canyon.

'Shit, kid,' Monty said. 'You can't even wipe your own ass. You gotta call some dollar-a-day waddie to clean up your goldam messes. You ain't got what it takes and your old man knows it. That's why he wants you to spark Ellen Watson. She could save the H Bar H for him. But you? I hear you like men better'n women.'

The kid came in punching, and Monty laid him out. Had to give the boy credit. He got up and came in again, swinging a chair.

Monty kicked young Billings's legs out from under him and connected with a looping right as he tried to get up. Smashed the boy's nose. Monty pushed the fight, slowly beating the kid to a pulp as he backpedalled all the way to the bar.

''Nuff,' Hollard Smythe, the bartender, said. 'Things'll go hard enough as it is. Lay off.'

The kid crumpled.

'I hear you, Holly,' Monty said. He picked up his new black hat, cleaned the sawdust off it, and set it on his head at a jaunty angle. He walked for the batwings and the kid had to shoot at

4

him. A man naturally shoots back and Hartley Billings lay dead.

'Jayzus,' Holly said. 'Old Man Billings'll be after your ass, Monty. You'd better light a shuck.'

Monty did. And now he had to decide whether to keep running. He never was one to run. Wasn't like him. He walked Baron down the hill and into Mexican Hat.

A dumpy stop on the outlaw trail, Mexican Hat bore the name of a rock formation off to the west, marking the eastern edge of Monument Valley. One saloon, one cantina, and a rickety place without windows that stood empty, but wore a faded sign that read: Garrison's General Store. Monty counted the hovels. Thirteen looked lived-in, half a dozen abandoned.

He walked Baron the sorrel down the trail — it would be hard to say a wagon road led into Mexican Hat — with the sun climbing near its zenith. Heat waves formed a mirage of cool water over the southern horizon. Sideless brush jacals kept the harsh sunlight from tiny patches of red dirt. A lizard panted, halfway up a bare juniper pole. Monty pulled his black Stetson low over his eyes. Without showing any sign, he searched the little village for anything unusual. A dog lay at the edge of the street, tongue lolling. The dirt around it said the dog was in its usual place.

Two horses stood before a low adobe structure that had CANTINA white-washed on one side. The whitewash was nearly gone, but the name was still readable. Twenty yards away, facing the cantina, a false-front frame building wore a sign that said: Whiskey. One horse stood hipshot in front of it. Nothing moved. Not even flies.

Half a mile on down the dusty track, a rickety bridge spanned the San Juan river. Maybe the only reason the town existed. It certainly was about the only place where cows and ponies could be swum across the San Juan and pushed down the trail toward Chinle, Juan

Lorenzo Hubbell's trading post, and Navajo Springs, where the thirsty stock could at last get a decent drink. Commodore Owens always had a bottle for the cowboys at his place there, and he never asked leading questions.

Monty chose the saloon. He could drink mescal when worse got to worst, but preferred a civilized drink, like branded whiskey: Old Grand-Dad, or Turley's Mill. Maybe he'd have time for a snort or two before Billings and his iron-toting men rode in.

He tied Baron to the hitching rail next to a brown that looked like it hadn't had a square meal or a chance to browse in the last month, maybe more.

There was no door, just an opening in the false front. Windows on either side gaped without panes, like the empty eye-sockets of a longhorn's skull. Monty shrugged.

Inside the saloon, Monty stepped aside and waited till his eyes could adjust to the dim interior. A quick glance showed him the scene. Dust on the floor. Dust on the chairs and tables. Dust on the empty bottles behind the bar. An old man with a scraggly beard stood with his back against the wall beyond the bar. Monty walked slowly over. He took the kerchief from around his neck and flapped it at the bar, moving enough dust for a place to put his elbows, which he did.

'Whiskey,' he said.

The old man shuffled over. 'I'd sell you house whiskey,' he said, his voice sounding like his throat was full of sandpaper, 'but I ain't got none. You'll have to make do with Old Potrero or Jameson's.'

'Old Potrero's good,' Monty said.

The old man squatted and rustled around in the space back of the bar. He stood up with a clear bottle in his hand. 'Knew I had some left,' he said. The bottle bore no sign of a label. The liquid in it was amber.

The man blew the collected sand and dust out of a shot glass and poured it brim full. 'That'll be a dollar,' he said.

'A dollar!'

'Yep.'

'Shee-it. Get four drinks for a dollar over to Woodrow's in Watsonville.'

'This ain't Watsonville. You can move across to the cantina. They may have some mescal. Most likely tiswin, though. A dollar.'

Monty paid.

The old man set the glass in front of him and put the bottle back under the bar.

'Whose cayuse outside?' Monty asked.

'Mine. Keep him there to draw customers. Mostly it works.'

'They got two in front of the cantina,' Monty said.

'White men usually want whiskey. One horse's enough.'

'Looks like he could use a good bait of oats.'

The old man cackled. 'Mister, you think a shot of whiskey's steep at a dollar, try buying a sack of oats. Me and that cayuse've been over more than one trail together. He gets fed afore me.'

Monty picked up the shot glass. 'Mud in your eye,' he said, and tossed the whiskey. His eyes watered and the liquor burned its way down his throat and into his stomach. He knuckled his watering eyes. 'Damn,' he said.

⋆ ⋆ ⋆

Ellen Watson rode hard, and Deputy US Marshal Cameron Slade was pressed to keep up with her. She rode a long-legged buckskin gelding with black mane and tail and long black stockings. She called him Sweetie.

Behind Ellen and the marshal, riders strung out along the trail. Jim Blakely, foreman. Chunky Willis, wrangler and horse breaker. Stem Douglas, dollar-a-day cowboy. And the Kid.

Billings led a dozen riders, Ellen figured, but she had a deputy US marshal who'd gotten the story of the Billings boy's shooting from Holly the bartender, who'd seen it all at first hand. 'Sounds like self-defense to me,' Slade said, 'but let's bring McCord in. Easier to protect him in jail, and when Judge Perkins pronounces him not guilty, Billings has got no leg to stand on.'

'Billings never needed legality,' Ellen said. 'He's always ridden roughshod over weaker people, and he won't stop now. At least, that's my opinion.'

She saddled Sweetie and called four good men. 'Monty's in a bind,' she said. 'He rides for this brand and we'll go get him out. Load for bear. Six-guns and saddle guns. Plenty of cartridges for both. Sing Chow will put together grub for five days. Pick it up.' Ellen Watson never asked her riders to do anything she wouldn't do herself, and they never called her anything but boss.

'Riders ahead,' Blakely said.

'I see the dust,' said Ellen. She rode Sweetie astraddle, like any cowboy, and she wore her curly hair cut short. 'Can't use up good ranching time fooling with my hair,' she always said. At the moment she had a light-brown Stetson pulled down around her ears and from the shade of the wide brim, her hazel eyes threw sparks. Nobody laid a hand on a Flying W rider without paying a price. That was the rule Frank Watson lived by, and Ellen felt the same.

The Flying W riders didn't catch up with the H Bar H bunch before they reached Mexican Hat, and when Ellen and her men topped the hogback, horses stood two deep, ground-tied in front of the saloon.

'Don't look like the necktie party's started yet,' Slade said.

'They've probably got Monty under the gun,' Ellen said, 'and no doubt some big cowpoke's beating on him.' She patted the sawed-off Parker hanging from her saddle horn. 'I'll go in the front door, Marshal. You can follow, if you please. Jim, take the Kid and come in the back. Chunky, Stem, you all follow me and the marshal in, but spread out to the side as soon as you get through the door. Chunky to the left. Stem to the right. Short range. Don't worry about rifles. Use your six-guns. OK. Let's move.'

Ellen Watson rode off the humpback and into Mexican Hat at a walk, sawed-off Parker on her thigh and a deputy US marshal at her side.

★   ★   ★

Monty paid another dollar for another drink and had the shot glass in his hand when H Bar H riders came through the door. Monty knew them all. A man didn't ride the line in Twin Forks Basin for long without learning every face that belonged on the range.

They came in with six-guns in their hands.

Monty downed his drink. 'You all must be plumb scared of little old me,' he said, and plonked the glass on the bar.

'Keep your hands away from the Colt, Monty.'

13

'Sure, Croft. Ain't never been one to jump into a fight where the odds're too far against me. What've we got here? Ten to one? Twelve?'

'Shut up.'

'What for? You gonna shoot a man for talkin'? Never did hear of a rowdy gettin' talked to death.'

'I said, shut up,' the man named Croft said, teeth clenched. 'The Old Man's coming in.'

Monty McCord grinned and turned his back on the H Bar H riders. 'Say, old man, never did get your name.'

'Norm,' he said. 'Bently Norm.'

'Well, then, Bently Norm. I've got another dollar, have you got another shot of Old Potrero? If you do, I'd admire to buy it from you.'

Norm's Adam's apple skittered up and down his neck.

'Monty McCord!' The roar sounded like an old mossy horn back in the pear thickets.

Monty turned. 'Good day to you, too, Mr Billings. I was about to have me

14

a slug of Old Potrero. Buck a shot. Be honored if you'd care to join me.'

'*Gee zus kee ryst*. You fired the goldam bullet that killed my son. You did that, and you have the gall to stand there and offer to buy me a drink?'

Monty pulled at his moustache and grinned. 'Mr Billings. When a man gets shot at in this country, he's got the right to shoot back. Your snot-nosed boy took a potshot at me. And that's not all. He was shooting at my back, almighty Hunter Billings. At my back! So all there is to say about your dead boy is this — he was a back-shooter.'

Hunter Billings growled deep down in his throat. His cowboys, pistols in hand, looked at him for orders.

'Take his gun,' Billings said.

Monty stood quiet while a cowboy plucked his Peacemaker from its holster.

'Hold him.'

Two burly cowboys braced Monty McCord. 'Sure would like another shot of Old Potrero,' he said.

15

Norm nodded and filled Monty's glass.

'Much obliged,' Monty said. 'Just a minute,' he said to the big men beside him. He half-turned, picked up the shot glass, and tossed the amber liquor back.

'Damned if that ain't prime whiskey.' Monty dug in his pocket for a cartwheel and put it on the bar. He turned all the way around to face Hunter Billings. 'Do your damndest,' he said.

The big cowboys took hold of Monty's arms.

Hunter Billings pulled on a pair of doeskin gloves, taking his time and making threatening glares. He cocked a fist and stepped in to slug the Flying W cowhand.

Monty McCord waited for just the right timing and kicked Hunter Billings square in the balls.

2

Hunter Billings collapsed, clutching his battered gonads. He retched up the morning's coffee with bits that may have been biscuits.

Monty didn't wait to see what would happen. He pivoted left, tearing his right arm loose and driving a fist into the stomach of the cowboy at his left. The fist smashed into the soft spot just below the breastbone. That freed his other arm.

Billings, on his hands and knees, barfed up more coffee.

'Wah hoo,' Monty hollered. 'You all think ten H Bar H rannies can take a Flying W waddie, you got another think a-coming.' He got a hand on the back of a heavy old chair. He lifted the rickety old thing and whirled around, holding it out at arm's length. The chair flew from his hands, spinning into the cowboys bunched up beside Nelson Croft, the H Bar H foreman. It took two men off their feet and down on the floor.

Monty laughed. A cowpoke smashed a fist into his ear. It split and blood flecked the side of his face. He hollered, 'Yee-e-e-haw, I'm king of the mountain and I ain't got started yet. Come and get what I'm givin' out, y'all.' To him, there was nothing quite as good as a knock-down drag-out brawl.

He grabbed a cowboy by the shirt front and reared back to give him a head butt in the face. Then someone fired both barrels of a shotgun.

Everyone froze.

'Cameron Slade, deputy US marshal,' a deep voice said.

'Shit, Marshal, we was just getting into it,' Monty said, still grinning. But a look of relief came to his face when he noticed Ellen Watson standing a little behind the marshal, smoke coming from the twin barrels of her sawed-off Parker. ''Lo, boss,' he said.

'Monty McCord. I only want to hear one thing from you. Tell me why in hell you ran off instead of coming to the Flying W.'

Monty studied the scuffed toes of his boots.

Jim Blakely and the Kid stood just inside the rear door, Colts in hand, hammers cocked. 'Croft,' Blakely said, 'you know me well. I'm asking you to have your men holster them hoglegs. We'll do things like Marshal Slade wants 'em done.'

'Sumbitchin' McCord kicked Mr Billings in the balls,' Croft said.

Blakely gave him a faint smile. 'How long you known Monty McCord, Croft? Three, four years? You ever hear of him going peaceful? That man was born to fight. You know that.'

Hunter Billings groaned.

'Sure glad I don't have balls,' Ellen said.

Monty laughed. 'Boss, you got more *cojones* than all the H Bar H men put together. That's a fact.'

Billings groaned again. 'Think something's busted,' he rasped.

Marshal Slade squatted beside Billings. 'Mr Billings,' he said, 'we're taking Monty McCord back to Watsonville for trial.'

'For trial?' Monty snorted. 'What the hell for? Since when does a man go to trial for defending himself?'

'Since you shot Hunter Billings's only son,' Slade said. His face hardened and his voice took on an edge. 'Miss Watson says you're a good line rider, McCord. Others say you're a hell-raiser who don't much care what gets broke or who gets cut or shot, just so long as there's a good fight and you come out alive.'

'You got me pegged, Marshal. What's that got to do with a trumped-up trial?'

'You killed a boy, McCord. A boy — '

Monty cut in. 'Hold on one goldam minute. That little kid had a Colt .45 — snub-nosed but a .45 — in his hand and his little pink finger pulled a trigger and sent a bullet after me when my

20

back was turned.'

'Heard all about it from Holly,' Slade said. 'But we gotta have a trial to keep Hunter Billings from hanging you.'

Billings moaned. 'Hang sumbitch anyways,' he said in a scratchy whisper. 'Ain't no one shoots a Billings and walks away scot free.'

'McCord's gonna stand trial, Mr Billings. Let's do this thing right.'

'Right. Wrong. Ain't nothing bringing Hartley back.' Maybe Billings's balls were recovering. His voice sounded stronger.

'Mr Croft, help Mr Billings to his feet. We'll leave as soon as he's ready to ride,' said the marshal.

'I ain't yet got my shot of Old Potrero,' Monty said. 'Hold on.' He stepped back to the bar. 'Norm, you oughta dust this place once in a while. Couldn't hurt. Might do good.' He clicked a silver dollar on to the bar. 'One for the road, OK?'

Norm poured the whiskey and took the dollar. Monty slugged it down.

'Man. That stuff's sure ain't Injun likker. Damn good.' He shot a sideways glance at Ellen Watson. 'Well, boss. What say we ride back to Twin Forks Basin?'

Ellen Watson stood back and let Marshal Slade handle matters. Monty McCord was a hell-raiser, no two ways about it. Papa Frank had hired him and he always did more than his share. He rode for the brand and was loyal to a fault. Ellen couldn't fathom why he'd run off after shooting Hartley Billings. Something didn't set right.

Marshal Slade got a promise from the H Bar H foreman, Nelson Croft, that there would be no gunplay. Hunter Billings sat in a chair now, but his pale face said his nuts still throbbed. Ellen stifled a smile. Men were so vulnerable, in so many ways.

'Monty, get your cracker ass out of this saloon and onto that sorry horse of yours,' Ellen said. She turned for the door, then looked over her shoulder.

Monty McCord still stood with his back to the bar, leaning on his elbows. She whipped around to face him. 'Look here, cowboy. I'm not talking just to hear my teeth rattle. Come on!'

Monty shook his head. 'I reckon not, boss. This here's my affair and mine alone. The bullet what killed Hartley Billings came from my .45. I was on the town, so none of what I done had nothing to do with the Flying W. Begging your pardon.'

'Get on your horse, McCord,' Slade said. 'I'll keep your gun.'

'Right away, Marshal. And don't you be giving that shooting iron to Miss Watson. She's not involved in this thing.' Monty heaved himself to his feet and strode to the door. As he passed Ellen, he said, 'Leave it lie, boss. Things'll go better that way.' He gave her a little smile and went out into the heat of the day.

Ellen heaved a sigh. Monty McCord never refused an order. He never even turned down a request. Maybe there was more to the shooting than she knew.

She went outside. Sweetie stood exactly where she'd ground-tied him. She rubbed his nose and he tossed his head. She pulled a spongy piece of carrot from her pocket to reward him for being such a good horse. He smelled it, nibbled at it, then crunched the vegetable between strong teeth, nodding his pleasure.

Slade waited for Monty to reach his horse before getting on his own.

H Bar H riders grouped around Hunter Billings, who sat his steeldust gelding with most of his weight on the right-hand stirrup. Apparently Monty's kick had robbed him of the ability to sit up in the saddle. Ellen forced herself to keep a straight face.

'You all move on ahead,' Slade said to Nelson Croft. 'We'll wait a while so you can get a good start. Don't want H Bar H cowpokes mixing with Flying W men right now. Move on out.'

'Let's go,' Croft hollered, and H Bar

H horses walked out of Mexican Hat, headed toward Twin Forks Basin.

Bently Norm stood in the doorway of his saloon and watched the riders leave. 'First good bunch of drinkers I've seen in a long time,' he said, more to himself than to anyone who might be listening. 'Sold each of them a drink and I'da been set for the winter. Shit.'

'Hang on a minute, Marshal.' Monty sauntered back to the door of the saloon. He dug in his pocket. 'I reckon you had nearly twenty drinkers in your saloon, Norm. I'd like to buy them all a drink.' He gave Norm a gold eagle. 'Dollar a shot. Twenty shots. Now. If ever one of them rannies comes into your place again, the first drink's on me. OK?'

Norm cackled. 'A goldam gold eagle,' he said. 'Goldarned eagle.'

Monty took his own sweet time getting back to Baron, and when he did, he made a big show of checking surcingles and cinches and such.

'You about ready, McCord?' Slade's voice dripped with exasperation.

'Man's got to be sure of his equipment before heading out, Marshal,' Monty said.

'I oughta tie you to your saddle horn,' Slade said.

Monty grinned. 'Well, I suppose you could arrest me. But then again, I ain't done nothing wrong, and a good lawman like Cam Slade wouldn't arrest someone like that, would he?'

Slade said nothing, but the exasperation on his face spoke loud and clear. 'On your horse,' he said. His tone of voice brooked no sass from Monty McCord.

'Yessir,' Monty said, and swung aboard Baron. 'Let's us ride on up the road and see if Judge Perkins figures I'm worth hanging.'

'Move it, McCord.'

'Go, Baron,' Monty said, and the sorrel obediently turned and followed the Flying W riders up the trail toward Twin Forks Basin.

Barry Seagle sat at his usual table in the Bucket of Blood. *Damn*. Hartley Billings went and got himself shot dead. Seagle shuffled the deck and dealt cards to the others at the table. He automatically shut out the babble of drinkers and the shrill laughter of the Bucket's whores. *Damn*. Seagle wondered if the markers he held from young Billings would be leverage enough to get himself into Hunter Billings's operation. Billings was gobbling Twin Forks Basin alive, and Seagle wanted in on the feast.

'Holly!' A whore two tables away hollered for the bartender. 'Hey Holly!'

'I ain't your servant,' the 'keep replied.

'Shut up and bring us another bottle,' she hollered, and cackled at the drummer setting beside her. Seagle could see the drummer was already pie-eyed drunk and knew he'd be rolled for everything he owned before the sun rose.

Holly the barkeep stalked over to the whore's table with a long-necked bottle full of amber liquid. Probably grain alcohol with tobacco for coloring and McIlhenny's tabasco sauce for bite. If a man was drunk enough, he couldn't tell the difference, and this one looked prime.

'Ten bucks,' Holly said.

'Pay the man, honey,' the whore said.

'Ten bucks?' The drummer looked at the bottle with studied concentration.

'Pay the man,' the whore said. 'I'll make it up to you later. More than make it up to you. Much more.'

The drummer's eyes were fixed on the whore's bulging bosom. He nodded and fumbled for his wallet. The whore's greedy eyes watched every move. She licked her lips and clutched the drummer's arm to the bosom he'd been watching. He pulled the arm away to extract a bill from the wallet.

'Ten dollars,' he said, and handed the bill to Holly.

'Thank you, sir. Have a good time.'

Holly put the full bottle on the table near two cloudy glasses, and took away the empty one, which bore a label. Seagle couldn't read it, but it looked like Turley's Mill. Respectable, and more than enough to dull a man's taste buds.

'Hit me,' said one of the players.

Seagle dealt him a card and took his discard.

'Young Billings got himself killed here a couple of nights ago,' the man said to no one in particular.

'What's it to you, Crum?' a stick-thin player said.

'Well, nothing particular. Just . . . Well, it were a bit strange,' the man called Crum said. He put a quarter in the pot.

'A quarter?'

'That's all the cards'll support,' Crum said. ''Sides, there ain't no limit on what a fellow can bet in this game.' He flicked a glance at Seagle. 'Right, Bear?'

Seagle gave Crum a hint of a smile.

'Twenty-five cents'll buy you five beers,' he said. 'No reason it can't buy you into a friendly little card game.'

'Say,' Crum said. 'What was you and young Billings talking about before he up and took that shot at Monty McCord?'

Seagle gave Crum a sharp look. 'Me? I was just seeing if there was something I could do for the dumb kid. 'Tweren't nothing important.'

'That so?' Crum took another peek at his cards. 'You in this round, Dan'l?'

Daniel Thorne, the stick-thin man, cleared his throat. 'Ahem. Well. I reckon for now, anyway.' He shoved a quarter out. 'I'll see you,' he said, 'and raise you a quarter.' He pushed another coin out to join the first.

'High rollers. That's what you gents are,' Seagle said. A grin showed on his face, but it came nowhere near his eyes. Crum White, at least, had noticed him say something to young Billings. Still, no one could say he'd egged the kid on. 'There he goes,' Seagle'd said to the

30

boy. 'That man just beat you to a pulp and you're gonna let him walk out of here like that?'

The boy took the hideout Seagle had in his hand, turned, and shot at McCord. He was supposed to hit the Flying W rannie dead center, but the best he could do before he died was nick McCord's ear. And that was enough to get him killed. Seagle had jumped to the boy's side the moment he went down, as much to get his hideaway as to help the kid. 'He's gone,' Seagle'd said, slipping the gun away. 'Hartley Billings's gone.'

'Jaysus,' Holly'd said. 'Old Man Billing'll be after your ass, Monty. You'd better light a shuck.'

McCord'd run out, jumped on his pony, and thundered away. Then Hunter Billings took a gaggle of riders and went after him. Seagle smiled. Monty McCord was a goner. One less bothersome fly in the ointment of his plans for Watsonville.

3

Nelson Croft, the H Bar H foreman, stood by the door to the marshal's office when Cameron Slade rode up with Monty McCord, Ellen Watson, and four Flying W cowboys in tow.

'Joe Butler in?' Slade said.

Croft thumbed at the door.

'I'da figured Hunter Billings'sd be here to watch me lock Monty McCord in a cell.'

'Sore nuts,' Croft said, deadpan.

Monty grinned. 'Nothing like boot leather to the balls,' he said. 'Shortens the odds lots a times.'

'Shut up, McCord,' Slade said, swinging his right leg over the cantle and dismounting. 'Get off that dumb cayuse and get into the marshal's office.

'Who's gonna take care of Baron? He don't sleep well 'less I tuck him in at night.'

'Shee-it, rannie. Ain't no one can spin a tall one like you. In.' Slade motioned at the door.

Monty grinned again. 'Boss,' he said to Ellen Watson, 'could you make sure Baron's looked after? He's a good pony. Shouldn't be long until I'm outta here.'

'You can trust the Flying W, Monty. You know that.'

'I do, boss, but sometimes people forget other people's horses.'

Ellen held a straight face, barely. 'Baron'll be all right,' she said.

Monty nodded, handed her Baron's reins, and stepped up on to the porch of the marshal's office.

Croft hadn't moved. He stood to the left of the door, one foot against the wall and thumbs hooked in his waistband.

Monty paused at the door. 'Figured you'd be out on the range where you can do some good, Croft. You are a cowman, ain't ya?'

'I am,' Croft said. 'And I'll make a

steer outta you if the boss don't heal right.'

Monty shrugged. 'Self-defense,' he said. 'Do your damndest.' He followed Cam Slade into the marshal's office. Croft didn't go in, but Ellen Watson did.

'Monty McCord?' Joe Butler, marshal of Watsonville, stood up when Marshal Slade entered with Monty a step behind. ''Lo Miss Watson,' he said when Ellen came in, too.

'I heard about Monty killing that brat Hartley Billings,' Butler said. 'Sounds like self-defense to me.'

'I got the story,' Slade said. 'But Billings is out for blood. If the circuit judge says it was self-defense, then Billings won't have no legal peephole that'll let him hang McCord. Just trying to keep the peace. We'll hold him for the judge.' Slade held out his hand. 'Keys?'

Butler gave Slade a slow look, then opened a desk drawer and pulled out a ring with two keys on it. He gave the keyring to Slade. 'You staying to keep the H Bar H boys from killing McCord while he's in here?'

Slade looked almost startled. 'Me?'

'Yeah, you. He's your prisoner, ain't he?'

'I gotta go over to Gunnison.'

'So who's in charge of McCord?'

Monty stood silent.

Slade said nothing.

Butler put his hands on his hips and stared at Slade.

Ellen broke the silence. 'Monty will give his word not to run off. Let him out on . . . what was that word the lawyers use?'

'Cognizance?'

'Yes, let him out on his own cognizance, and I'll guarantee he's here when the judge comes. That's assuming you'll be here then, too, Marshal Slade.'

'What do you say, McCord?' Slade said.

'I'm just a line rider, Marshal. I do what my boss says. Always.'

Slade let out a big breath. 'I reckon

you're right on this one, Miss Ellen.' He gave Butler a nod, handed the keyring back, and turned to Monty. 'You promise to come into town and stand up in front of Judge Perkins when he gets here?'

'I can do that,' Monty said.

'Miss Ellen, you figure Monty McCord'll be better off at the Flying W?'

'Don't know about better off, Marshal, but he won't be causing Joe Butler any grief. Joe's a good man and he does a lot to keep Watsonville peaceful. Cowboys on the town know if they get rowdy, they'll end up in Joe's hoosegow and have to pay a fine. Ten, fifteen dollars bites into a cowboy's pay pretty deep. Anyway. Yes. I think Monty will be better off at the Flying W, and I put my promise up with his. I'll make sure Monty McCord is here when Judge Perkins sets up court.'

Monty scuffed a toe at the rough planking of the floor. He kept his eyes on his boot.

'All right,' Slade said. 'McCord, you're a lucky sumbitch. I'll take your word on it. But don't go shooting up half the H Bar H ranch hands while you're waiting.' He waved a hand at the door. 'Get outta here.'

Monty grinned. 'Gladly. Boss, can we go home now?'

'We can,' Ellen said, and led the way back to the street.

'McCord's going free?' Nelson Croft stood in the same place, one foot propped against the wall.

'Not free, Croft,' Monty said. 'Just not to jail. I gave my word to show up when Judge Perkins comes to town. You know I ain't never broke my word, and I ain't gonna start now. Not over a snot-nose brat like Hartley Billings.'

'He'll be at the Flying W,' Ellen said. 'I've got plenty of work for him to do. It's not like he's getting time off or something.'

'We'll be watching,' Croft said.

'Watch away. You won't see nothing.' Monty stepped off the porch and untied Baron. 'Let's be going, boss. If you please.'

Flying W hands mounted and rode southwest out of town. Monty glanced back at the jail just before they turned the corner. Croft was gone.

★　★　★

Hunter Billings lay in the darkness, his eyes wide open.

Damn Monty McCord.

It throbbed down there between his legs. Throbbed and ached and the pain spread upwards into his guts.

Damn, damn, and double damn McCord.

Billings stifled a groan. He had a ranch to run and a town to look after. Couldn't let a little pain get him down. Couldn't let a kick to the balls put him away. Had to get up and get going.

His bladder told him he needed to pee. But that meant climbing out of bed, pulling the chamber pot from under it, and getting down on his knees to dribble piss into the goldam pot. Dribble. There was a day when he'd step out the back and release a healthy stream at the juniper tree. Like a stallion. Shit. A goldam dribble.

The old man crawled from under the down comforter that warded off early-morning chill. His feet came down on a rag rug hooked by the wife who'd left him with a young boy to raise when influenza swept through in '75.

He knelt and felt for the chamber pot. It seemed heavier than usual. Then he remembered dribbling into it some-time in the night. He pulled it close and removed the wooden lid. He hung the poor excuse of what had been a manly pecker over the edge and dribbled. He closed his eyes and put his forehead against the bed. And dribbled.

Much later, his bladder empty but the pain in his crotch unreleased, Billings managed to put the lid back on the chamber pot and push it under the bed. He struggled to his feet. *Must get up. Must get things done. Must . . .*

Billings fell face down across the bed. He didn't move.

'Massa? Massa?' Ching Lee, the cook, stood in the doorway.

Billings groaned.

'Massa?'

Ching Lee disappeared. Billings groaned again. And again. Then Ching Lee returned with Nelson Croft in tow.

'Boss?' Croft put a hand on Billings's shoulder. 'Boss? You OK?'

Billings moaned. 'Goldam hurts,' he said, his voice no more than a hoarse whisper.

'Your balls still banged up?'

'Hurts.'

'Geez. Let's get you straight on the bed.' Croft and Ching Lee wrestled Billings around and covered him with the comforter.

Billings groaned.

Ching Lee and Croft left the bedroom.

'Ching Lee, you watch the boss. Get some whiskey into him, as much as you can. That'll stop him from hurting so much. I'll see if I can get some help.'

'Yes, Massa Nels. I watch. I help,' Ching Lee said.

Croft caught a black-legged bay from among the horses in the home corral, saddled up, and rode. No doctor had ever put out his shingle in Watsonville. The nearest hospital was at old Fort Defiance, nearly a hundred miles south.

*   *   *

Somehow Croft's bay took the trail over a ridge and through a cut to the Flying W ranch. It wasn't as if Croft planned it that way, but the bay seemed to have a mind of its own and Croft gave the gelding its head. He thought and he thought. When it came to first-calf heifers or old mossy horns stuck in the bog, no one was better than Nelson Croft at doing the right thing. Organizing a round-up, branding the spring calf crop, making sure the herd had enough salt . . . name a ranch job and Nelson Croft did it better than most. But now his boss was down and hurting. A man might have tender nuts for a few days after a kick in the balls, but Croft figured Hunter Billings had something else wrong. Something deep inside. He didn't know what to do and his horse took him to the Flying W.

The sound of a lever jacking a shell into a saddle gun brought Croft back to the present.

'Where in hell do you think you're going?' a hard voice said.

'I need to talk to Miss Ellen,' Croft said. He kept his hands on the saddle horn. Now was not the time for gunplay.

A cowboy stepped from the open barn door. 'H Bar H's riding hard after one of us, Croft. Coming after him when all he done was defend hisself.' The speaker stood tall and slim, and he held a Winchester '73 like a pistol in his right hand, the hammer fully cocked.

'I'm not after McCord, Swift. I just need to talk to Miss Ellen.'

Swift mounted the steps to the porch,

took two long strides, and rapped on the door. The muzzle of the Winchester never strayed from pointing at Croft's chest.

'That's enough, Gerry,' Ellen said. 'Mr Croft's not here as an enemy.'

'Never know about them H Bar H rannies,' Swift mumbled. Still, he lowered the Winchester and let the hammer down. 'You touch my boss, Croft, and you'll have me to answer to.' He turned and strode back toward the barn, his back stiff with disapproval.

'You've got loyal men, Miss Ellen,' Croft said.

Ellen smiled. 'Get down and come in, Nels. I'll not bite, and no Flying W rider will assault you unless I give the word.'

'Yes, ma'am.' Croft swung a leg over the cantle and dismounted. He looped the bay's reins over the hitching rail, then unbuckled his gunbelt and hung his old converted dragoon on the saddle horn.

'No need to do that, Nels,' Ellen said.

'Wouldn't want any Flying W men getting the wrong idea,' Croft said. He climbed the steps to the porch and stood for a moment, searching Ellen's eyes.

She smiled. 'Come,' she said.

Croft nodded, but held back until Ellen went inside ahead of him.

Inside, Ellen turned. 'Nels, I don't like what's going on. It's not fair to Monty, and it could blow Twin Forks Basin apart. Not to mention us.'

'El, you know I don't hold to this. I know Monty reacted to Hartley's shot from behind him. I know that. But the boy was the only thing the old man had. He didn't know about you and me, and figured there might be some way to get the brat hitched to you.'

'I know. I'm not blind. I could see through Hunter Billings's intent just as if he'd had it printed up on a poster. Now it all means nothing. Hartley's gone, and our outfits are on opposite sides of the same valley.' She reached out and put her hand on Croft's arm.

He steeled himself, told himself it would not be right to take her in his arms. A man never knew who might be watching. He cleared his throat. Words wouldn't come.

'What is it, Nels?'

'It's the old man,' he said.

'What about him?'

'Ever since Monty kicked him in the . . . '

'I think men say 'balls', Nels.' Ellen chuckled.

'Yeah. Well ever since Monty kicked the old man, he ain't been good. And this morning early, he was hurting bad. There ain't no doc in these parts, and, well, I don't know what to do. Thought you might.'

'I'm no doctor, Nels, but I'm happy to do what I can. You know I bear Hunter no ill will. But I won't let him hang Monty McCord.'

'That's not something I'm worried about right now,' Croft said.

'Do you mind if I ride over to see

Hunter, to talk to him? Would you take me?'

'I'd appreciate it, El. I really would.'

Ellen stepped to the door. 'Gerry,' she called. 'Gerry Swift.'

'Coming, boss.' A faint voice came from the direction of the barn. Then pounding boots, and a rap on the door.

Ellen opened it.

'What do you need, boss?'

'Please saddle Sweetie, and your own horse as well. We're going over to the H Bar H.'

Swift stood in stunned silence for a moment.

'Gerry! Move!' Ellen's voice took on an edge. 'And send Deerstone to see me.'

'Deerstone?' Croft raised his eyebrows.

'Sometimes Ute medicine really works,' Ellen said. 'It can't hurt to have the medicine man from Deerstone's village come to see Hunter.'

Croft couldn't say no: he didn't know anything better to do. 'Whatever you say, Miss Ellen,' he said. He couldn't let Swift hear him call her El. No one really knew about them. Not even the preacher at Watsonville's tiny church.

'Yo,' Swift said, and went off to carry out his boss's orders.

'Sit down, Nels,' Ellen said. 'It will take a few minutes to get ready. I'll get you a cup of coffee.' She disappeared into the lean-to kitchen and came back with a coffee pot and two thick pottery mugs. 'I'd get the good china out,' she said, 'but somehow I don't like to think of you as a guest.' Her smile was soft, and so were her eyes.

Croft stood at the table, unable to say anything to this woman, who seemed to return his feelings for her. He sat.

Ellen brushed against his shoulder as she poured the coffee. His heart jumped. She smiled, moved to the other side of the table, and poured coffee in her own mug. She lifted it to take a sip, never taking her eyes off his.

Croft cleared his throat again, not knowing what to say.

47

'Are you catching something? Croup?'

'Er. No. But . . . '

'But what?' Ellen said, her eyes sparkling with mischief.

'I'm having a hard time, just sitting here,' he said.

'I find it pleasing,' Ellen said. 'After all, I don't get an opportunity to sit across from you and feast my eyes very often.'

Croft ducked his head. Belatedly, he removed his hat and hung it on the ladder-back chair next to him. 'Sorry,' he mumbled. Then he had a thought.

'Say, El. I ain't seen Monty McCord around. Where's he at?'

'Monty? Oh, he's out riding the east-west line, doing what he does best.'

4

Monty'd left his new black Stetson hanging in the bunkhouse at the Flying W. It was a go-to-town hat anyway. The one that kept the sun out of his eyes while he rode the line was bleached of pretty near all of whatever color it had been. The crown carried a Montana crease and the brim flopped down front and back. Grease spots ran around the sweatband, honest oil from Monty's honest brow.

The Flying W ran its 10,000 head in the northern reaches of Twin Forks Basin, and the H Bar H ran something over 30,000 across the southern part. No fences separated the two spreads, and waterholes and haying pastures were about the only patented land the two ranches owned.

Monty rode the imaginary east-west line between the spreads. When he came across H Bar H stock, he shooed them back to the south. Once in a while he'd spy some Flying W beef on H Bar H range, and he'd ride over and chouse them back to the northern sections. He kept his eyes peeled for varmints. Mountain lions could down a calf. Wolves could even take a full-grown cow. Bears tended to stay away from live beef, but they'd make short work of a downed steer. But the worst varmints walked on two legs, threw a wide loop, and used a running iron — usually at night.

He came across the tracks of half a hundred beeves on his third morning riding the line. Cows don't travel in herds, except when some two-legged varmint bunches them up and keeps them that way. A cow will walk a long way to water, but other than that, she'll stay put as long as there's something to eat and somewhere to shade up.

Baron stopped at a tug on his reins, and Monty stared at those tracks. They were all on the H Bar H side of the line, and they were headed in a straight line for Biddle Pass, as if they were going to market.

Monty followed the trail for half a mile or so until another bunch joined up from the south. Had to be close to a hundred head, and the tracks were no more than a day old. No bunch of cows can outrun a determined cowboy on a tough pony. Monty took stock. Pistol and rifle chambered for .44–40. Twenty-five bullets in the gunbelt, five in the Colt revolver, fifteen in the saddle gun. An extra box in the offside saddle-bag. Still, one cowboy against half a dozen or more rustlers wasn't fair odds, even when the cowboy was Monty McCord.

In a split second Baron hit a full run, belly to the ground, making a beeline for the H Bar H ranch.

When Baron started heaving for breath, Monty slowed him to a trot. The H Bar H headquarters lay a good twenty miles to the west southwest, and no horse could do that distance at a dead run. After Baron got his wind, Monty lifted him into an easy lope that ate up the distance, but didn't break a horse's wind.

Long after sundown, Monty walked Baron toward the H Bar H ranch house. No Indian trouble and no range war, so that meant no one was on lookout. A low light in the bunkhouse said most of the H Bar H men were in the sack.

Monty heaved himself from the saddle and looped Baron's reins over the hitching rail. Tired to the bone, he climbed the three steps to the porch and strode to the front door. As he raised his hand to knock, the door opened.

'Kee ryst. What in hell are you doing here?' Croft wasn't the belligerent man he'd been at the jail in Watsonville.

'Come to see you, Croft, and Old Man Billings,' Monty said.

'Boss's in bed, McCord. He ain't got over that kick in the balls yet.'

'No shit. Wouldn't think it'd take that long.'

Croft looked Monty in the eye. 'No, it shouldn't. It's something else, something downright serious. Miss Ellen's in there with him and Deerstone's brought some kind of medicine man from the Ute camp. Serious, McCord, damn serious.'

'I come with more bad news, too, I'd say. Come across tracks up there about five miles northwest of Kinlay Butte. Lots of beef tracks, Croft. Looked to me like someone was driving off a hundred head of H Bar H cows. Figured you'd want to know.'

Croft straightened up. His eyes turned sharp and focused. 'Rustlers?'

'I'd say so.'

'We've lost the odd steer now and again. Usually someone hunting big antelope. But a hundred head . . . ' Croft took off his hat, ran his fingers through a mop of dark hair, and put the hat back on four square. 'Get an idea of how many riders was pushing the beef?'

'I made out prints of four different cayuses. Probably more, though.'

'You didn't take out after them?'

'Not my cows, Croft. Figured you'd decide what to do. Be glad to ride with you, if you want.'

'Not on that horse. If they're pushing a hundred head of beef, they ain't going fast. There's a empty stall in the barn where you can put your horse if you want. Plenty of feed and grain. Help yourself. Come on into the kitchen when you're set. I'll have cookie whip up some grub for you.'

'You going after them?'

'Come first light.'

'Lend me a horse, Croft. I'll ride to the Flying W and come back with Chunky and the Kid. They're as good as they come when the shooting starts.'

'I can do that; take your pick of the nags in the rear corral, but you'd better talk to your boss afore you go.'

Monty went to set Baron up in the barn while Croft told the boys in the bunkhouse what was going on. The seven horses in the corral weren't happy about Monty, a stranger, coming after them, but he had a loop on a piebald paint in short order. Once the rope pulled up on the paint, he settled down and Monty got him into the barn and saddled without any fuss.

Croft walked in as Monty got set to mount up. 'See ya got Old Pie,' he said.

'Old Pie, eh?'

'What else would you call a piebald pony?'

'Elwood, maybe?'

Croft barked a laugh. 'McCord, you got to be the strangest cowhand I ever come across. I swear.'

Monty climbed aboard the paint. 'Reckon I'll see the boss now. Tell her what's going on.'

'Good.' Croft strode ahead of Monty and went into the house.

Monty reined Ole Pie up in front of the house. A moment later, Ellen Watson opened the door and came out on to the porch. Croft stopped at the open door.

'Monty?'

' 'Lo, boss. Looks like rustlers. H Bar H stock, a hunnert head or so. I'll ride to the Flying W for Chunky and the Kid. Then we'll go with Croft and his cowboys to chase them owlhoots down. Your permission, of course.'

'Rustlers? The range has been quiet since I was a little girl. Why would rustlers hit now?'

'Someone spotted a weakness, most likely,' Croft said. 'We ain't been riding the range like we used to.'

'Go on, Monty. Jim can do without those two. Tell him you saw me,' Ellen said.

'I'm off,' Monty said. He touched Old Pie with a spur and headed for the Flying W at a lope.

Old Pie carried Monty northwest at a steady pace, confirming Monty's eye for horseflesh — lots of bottom if not a great beauty. They loped through the Flying W gate in the dead of night. Monty reined Old Pie up at the hitching rail in front of the ranch house.

'You'd better be friendly.' The hard voice was punctuated by the *click-click* of a six-gun being cocked.

'Jay-zus, Fred. Why in hell are you throwing down on me?'

'That you, Monty? Hell, you know I don't see good as I used to. Where's Baron?'

'Over to the H Bar H.'

'But . . . but . . . but them rowdies was fixing to hang you.'

'May yet, but first we got rustlers to catch. Where's Jim?'

'Where d'you expect? Sawing logs.'

'Could you water Old Pie here, Fred? He's come a ways. Maybe a bait of grain, too?'

'We-e-e-ll, I reckon.'

Fred led the paint off toward the watering trough and Monty plunged into the black innards of the bunkhouse. He reached for the storm lantern that hung inside the door and lit it with a lucifer. He trimmed the wick low and moved quietly to Jim Blake's bunk.

The instant Monty's hand touched Blake's shoulder, he found himself looking at the business end of a Remington Army. Blake let the six-gun's hammer down when he recognized Monty.

'Shee-it, man. Hadn't oughta put a hand on a man in the middle of the night. What the hell's going on?'

'Rustlers.'

'Wha-a-at?'

'They's driving a hunnert or so H Bar H beeves up toward Kinlay Butte.'

'So?'

'So Croft's gonna run 'em down. Starting at first light. I'm here for Chunky and the Kid. Boss said OK. Said you was to run things. Looks like Old Man Billings's got sumpin' wrong with him. More'n just a kick in the balls. Boss's over there helping out.'

'And them cowboys was ready for a shooting match with us over you.'

'Cain't have rustlers. Us or the H Bar H. We don't run these ones down, them out on the outlaw trail are gonna figure Twin Forks Basin as easy pickings.'

58

'Know that, damn it. Get your men and get the hell outta my sight.'

'Thanks, Jim.'

Monty woke Chunky and the Kid, and they were on the trail back to the H Bar H inside an hour. Old Pie held up fine, bolstered as he was with a long drink of water and a quart of good oats.

They rode hard and hit the H Bar H a good hour before dawn. The bunkhouse and the ranch house had lanterns lit and H Bar H cowhands were gearing up to chase rustlers.

Nelson Croft met the Flying W hands in front of the house. 'Chunky. Kid. Good of you all to come,' he said.

He turned to Monty. 'Your Baron horse has been eating us out of house and home. Hope he rides as good as he eats.'

The Flying W men dismounted and loosened the surcingles on their saddles.

'You'll be wanting to change horses,' Croft said. 'Take your pick of them in the corral. The boys brung some mounts in so we've got plenty.'

Seven cowboys rode out from the H Bar H ranch as the sky began to lighten beyond the Rockies to the east. Nelson Croft ramrodded the bunch and Monty McCord rode in the lead.

★   ★   ★

Barry Seagle didn't own a horse and he didn't own a buggy. Wherever he wanted to go in Watsonville, he walked, ramrod straight with long strides. But today, walking was not an option. Today, he would confront Hunter Billings with his son's gambling debts. Today was the first day of Barry Seagle's quest to take control of Watsonville, Twin Forks Basin, and if he was fortunate, the county, and then the state.

Hunter Billings owned much of Watsonville, but he paid little attention to the town. Once he was in charge, Barry Seagle would kick Watsonville into high gear. He'd lobby Hatch &

Hodges into running a weekly stage from Denver to Salt Lake City, stopping in Watsonville, of course. He'd hire prospectors — not old men with burros, but professional mineral hunters — because Watsonville needed more than beef if it was going to grow and prosper. Barry Seagle went over his plans for Twin Forks Basin as he drove his rented buggy from town to the H Bar H ranch, a distance of slightly more than seven miles.

No one greeted Seagle as he drove up. The ranch headquarters seemed almost dead. If it weren't for the chickens searching the yard for insects and bits of green, and a wisp of smoke rising from the chimney, he would have thought the place deserted.

He climbed out of the buggy, clipped a line to the mare's bit ring, and tied it to the hitching rail. Pausing at the steps to the porch, he smoothed his dove-gray coat and made sure its single button was fastened. He set his short-brimmed gray hat at just the right angle, removed his kid gloves, and held them in his left hand as he stepped up on to the porch. His pulse quickened. In a few minutes, he'd either be on his way to becoming one of the most influential men in Watsonville, or he'd have to go to his back-up plan.

Seagle took a deep breath and rapped on the front door. To his surprise, Ellen Watson opened it.

'Miss Watson. Who'd have thought you'd answer the door at the H Bar H?'

'Good day to you, too, Mr Seagle,' Ellen said. 'May I ask what brings you here?'

'I wish to speak with Mr Billings. I've a few things to discuss with him.'

'I'm afraid Mr Billings is indisposed.'

'Indisposed?'

'Quite.'

'No visitors, then?'

'I'm afraid not. Perhaps in a week or two.'

'What have you done to him? Are you after him because of Monty McCord?'

'Mr Billings is seriously ill and that

62

has nothing to do with either the Flying W or the H Bar H. Petty quarrels are set aside when neighbors get sick. You should know that.'

Seagle tipped his hat. 'Of course. Neighbors. Well. If I cannot see Hunter Billings, I'll just have to do my best on my own.' Seagle started to turn away, then looked back. 'Would you be so good as to give Mr Billings a note for me?'

'He's not in a condition to read at the moment, but if you wish to leave a missive, I will make certain he gets it the moment he's well enough. Have you anything to write with?'

'I have a tally book, but if there's a pen and ink and a sheet of foolscap in the house, I'd be grateful if I could use them.'

'Come in. Pardon my inhospitality.' Ellen stepped back to allow Seagle through the door.

The room surprised him. Billings might be the richest man in the Twin Forks Basin, but no one would know it by looking at the front room of the H Bar H ranch house.

Nothing wore the imprint of the States. No photos. No paintings. No Chippendale-style chairs. A small, tightly woven Navajo rug hung on the west wall. A fireplace dominated the south, with a pair of horse pistols on pegs above the mantel. Not a single hunting trophy, and the furniture was handmade of native Utah juniper lashed with rawhide. A battered roll-top desk sat in one corner, and a gun cabinet in the corner opposite. Seagle noted three long-barrel Winchesters, two Parker double-barreled shotguns, and a Hawken muzzleloader, of all things.

'Let me see if the writing implements are in the desk,' Ellen said, as if she owned the house.

'Obliged,' Seagle said.

She rolled up the top. 'All, yes. Quills. Ink. Paper.' Ellen returned with the implements in hand. 'You may compose your note at the dining table,' she said. 'I'll get a cup of coffee for you.'

Leaving the paper and ink on the table, Ellen disappeared into the kitchen. Seagle sat down to write, but before he could actually put pen to paper, Ellen returned with a cup and saucer in one hand and a large coffee pot in the other. She placed the cup and saucer at Seagle's left and poured the rich dark brew. 'Sugar? Cream?'

'A bit of cream would be welcome,' Seagle said.

'One moment.' She fetched a little pitcher of cream, set it next to the coffee, and left.

With a blank sheet of paper before him and a freshly trimmed quill and an ink bottle at his right hand, Seagle sipped at coffee so full of cream it looked almost gray. He set the cup down and picked up the quill. He dipped it into the ink and pulled the paper close. Then he wrote.

To Mr Hunter T. Billings, Esq.
This missive is to appraise you of the fact that I personally hold eight

thousand five hundred and thirty dollars ($8,530) in notes signed by your late son, Hartley Simpson Billings, in lieu of payment of amounts lost at the poker table. At your earliest convenience, may we speak of my taking over certain of your assets in the town of Watsonville as payment of said promissory notes?

I remain,
Sincerely yours,

Seagle signed the sheet with a flourish.

5

When Ellen returned to Hunter Billings's bedroom, Deerstone and Gerry Swift sat against the wall in ladder-back chairs. Billings opened his eyes as she entered. 'Goldam embarrassing to have a woman looking after what's wrong with me, Ellen.'

She smiled. 'What are neighbors for, Mr Billings, if not to help when needful?'

'I'm still gonna get that Monty McCord,' Billings said, his normally gruff voice now little more than a hoarse whisper.

'We'll cross that bridge when the time comes,' Ellen said. 'Right now, we must get you back on your feet.'

The Ute medicine man from Deerstone's people came into the bedroom with a steaming coffee pot in one hand and a ceramic mug in the other. He said something to Deerstone, who replied. Ellen saw the question in Deerstone's eyes. The medicine man spoke again, this time at some length.

Deerstone turned to Billings. 'Many Winters, our medicine man, says you should drink of this tea.'

'Why? All he done was pull down my eyelid and pinch my wrist and stick his finger up my bum. What does he know?'

Deerstone said something to Many Winters. The medicine man stared at Hunter Billings. He didn't blink. He didn't speak. Billings stared back. Finally Many Winters spoke, this time directly to Billings. Deerstone interpreted.

'Many Winters say the color of a man's eye, the white part, says many things about his insides. Yours say you drink too much whiskey. Maybe because you hurt. Hurt body. Hurt spirit.

'Many Winters say the beat of your heart, as he felt from holding your

68

wrist, is not steady like one who is strong of body and mind. Sometimes fast, sometimes slow, sometimes strong, sometimes weaker.

'Many Winters say there is a lump up inside you that he felt with his finger.' Deerstone held up his index finger to illustrate. 'He say sometimes that kind of lump goes away, sometimes a man with such a lump dies after much hurting.'

Deerstone said no more, and the medicine man held out the mug again.

Billings rasped a question. 'What's in the goldam mug?'

Deerstone asked Many Winters, then interpreted the answer. 'Many Winters say there is yellow uinta water lily powder in the tea. And bark of white birch. White willow bark. Peyote. Sage. That's all.'

'Next thing, you'll have me eating mushrooms and skunk cabbage,' Billings said, but he reached for the mug.

Many Winters nodded, handed Billings the mug, then went into a long soliloquy while looking first at Billings, then at Deerstone.

'Many Winters say the medicine will make your lump go down, maybe. Pee better after.

'Many Winters say the medicine will help take hurt away.

'Many Winters say must drink every morning and every night. He makes enough to drink one cup morning, night, for ten days, then he comes again. Maybe stick finger in bum, too.'

The medicine man watched as Billings downed the brew.

'Ye gads! The least you could do would be put some honey in this horse piss. Yuk.'

Deerstone said something to Many Winters, who replied.

'Many Winters say good medicine very bitter. Way enough is enough, too much is poison. Don't drink too much.'

'Thank you, Many Winters,' Ellen said. 'We will see that Mr Billings takes his medicine.' There was a twinkle in her eyes. 'We know some medicine is very bitter. Thank you.'

Deerstone interpreted.

Many Winters grunted, then nodded. 'White boss speak good words,' he said. 'We go,' he said to Deerstone. 'Come back ten days.' He held up both hands, fingers spread. He pointed an index finger at Billings. 'Come poke. Make medicine. You drink.' He stood staring at Billings for a long moment. 'Good,' he said. 'We go.'

'Damn,' Billings said. 'Coulda talked American the whole time.'

'Better not,' Many Winters said. 'We go. Come back.'

Ellen saw Deerstone and Many Winters to the door. 'Thank you again, Many Winters,' she said.

'Maybe he die,' Many Winters said. 'Maybe not.'

Ellen nodded. 'I know,' she said. 'You can go back to the Flying W, Deerstone. Gerry's more than enough here.'

'Yes, boss,' the Ute cowpuncher said. 'What do I tell Blakely?'

71

'Just what happened . . . what's happening.'

'OK.' The two Utes left the porch and walked toward the barn in loose-kneed, flowing strides. Ellen watched until they disappeared into the dark interior. A few moments later they rode out on three-colored paints so closely matched they almost looked like the same horse. As they went by, Ellen turned to go back to Billings's room. She remembered Seagle's note and retrieved it from the rolltop, still folded in three. Whatever the gambler had written concerned only Billings, and Ellen respected that.

Billings sat in bed with his back against pillows piled at the headboard. 'Damn Injun juice that shaman fixed me must work somewhat,' he said. 'Ain't hurting like before. Goldam Monty McCord. Kicking an old man in the balls like that.'

'Mr Billings, Mr Billings. Two of your cowboys had ahold of Monty and you were going to beat him up without thought of fairness or honor. I'd kick you in the balls, too, if you tried the same trick with me.' Ellen's smile took some of the sting from her words.

'Damn you, Ellen Watson. You're bad as your old man.' Billings shrugged but his face said he wasn't really angry.

'Barry Seagle was here a while ago. I said you were not likely to be able to see him today, so he left you this note.' She held the folded foolscap out.

'Seagle?'

'That's what I said.'

'Shit. Oh, pardon me, El. Ain't used to having a woman around. Lemme see.' He stuck out a work-hardened hand. Ellen passed him the note.

★   ★   ★

Monty McCord, Nelson Croft, and their band of rustler hunters came across sign of the drive in mid-morning. The Kid piled off his horse and shoved a cowpie with a boot toe. 'Day old,' he said, 'maybe more.'

'Pretty dry trail,' Croft said.

'We gotta follow it,' said Monty. 'Won't do to let people get away with driving off stock on the hoof, ours or yours.'

'Know that, McCord, but they've got a whurthy lead on us.'

Monty chewed on his moustache for a long minute, staring at the tracks of a hundred or so H Bar H cows. 'Croft, I'm thinking those owlhoots'll take the beeves to Denver. Gunnison's going bust and Salida is just a little place. Ain't nowhere else near enough, or big enough, for that many cows.'

'Could go to Fort Lewis. Agent there's always looking for beef.'

'Yeah, I reckon. So what do you say? Follow the trail? Break off and cover Denver and Fort Lewis? You're the boss, Croft. Your call.' Monty pulled the makings from a shirt pocket and started rolling a smoke.

'We ain't got the men to do it all.' Croft frowned in concentration. 'Right now, all we know's someone's driving beeves east. To Denver, they gotta go through Monarch Pass. To Fort Lewis, they've got to turn south.' He threw a glance at Monty. 'McCord, how 'bout you and the Kid making straight for Monarch? If the beeves ain't passed, hunker down and wait a day. If no beeves show, head south for Durango to hook up with us.'

'OK. Them beeves show and there ain't no army chousing 'em, me and the Kid'll get them back for you. Count on it.'

Monty and the Kid rode hard, alternating between a long lope and a fast walk to help the horses last. They reached No Name Creek at the mouth of the road over Monarch Pass as the evening light faded. 'Take a quick gander over the trail, Kid. See if there's been a bunch of beeves on it lately.'

'Yo,' the Kid said, and rode off toward the approach to the pass.

Monty found a place to set up camp for the night, a bunch of rocks pushing up through the grassy surrounds. The tallest of the rocks stood some thirty feet high, and formed an overhang. It would reflect the light and heat of their fire, if they chose to light one.

The Kid came back, walking his pony. 'They're here,' he said.

'Where at?'

'On a flat down the creek a ways. They'll hit the grade up the pass in the morning, I reckon.'

'Ya don't say.'

'Monty?'

'They in a position where we could hit 'em running?'

'Monty?'

'Always best to get cows up and running in the right direction right off. A good run — '

'Monty!'

Monty gave the Kid a sharp look. 'What?'

'It's Red Carlisle.'

Monty chewed on his moustache, then kicked at a clod. 'Red Carlisle?'

'Yup.'

'Shit.'

'Yup.'

'I reckon I'd better go reason with him.'

'Yup.'

'Well, a man's gotta do what he's gotta do. Ain't no other way.' He whistled Baron over and put the bit back between his teeth. 'Sorry, old son,' he said, 'but we gotta go palaver.'

He swung up onto the big sorrel's back and settled himself into the saddle. 'Lead the way, Kid,' he said.

The Kid reined away. Monty McCord followed, not happy at all about how things were going, and the cows didn't even wear the brand he rode for.

No Name Creek ran south out of the mountains and across grassy flats made green by its waters. Major Creek joined it about four miles from the campsite Monty had chosen. Red Carlisle had the H Bar H cows bedded down between No Name and Major, where there was only one way in and out.

'That's far enough,' a hard voice said.

The sound of a Winchester lever lifting a cartridge into the receiver punctuated the lookout's warning.

'Hands on the saddle horn, Kid,' Monty said. He raised his voice. 'Monty McCord here. Need to palaver with Red Carlisle.'

'Which side of the trail are you riding today, McCord?'

'You know me, Bud. I'm always on the side of the brand. Come on. Let me go talk to Red.'

'Gonna have to take your hardware, McCord. The Kid's, too.' The man called Bud stepped out from behind the thick trunk of a hundred-foot ponderosa.

'Don't want to drop these good guns on the ground, Bud. Can I just hand them to you? I'll get off ol' Baron real careful.'

Bud took a step back and put the Winchester to his shoulder. 'All right. Get off the pony. Slow and easy. You too, Kid.'

'Don't do nothing 'til we've talked to

Red,' McCord said to the Kid.

'One of him, two of us,' the Kid said.

'We got nothing to gain by killing him,' Monty said. 'We're here to talk.' He pulled his saddle gun from its scabbard and handed it to Bud. Then unbuckled his gun rig and did the same.

Bud held his Winchester in his right hand like a pistol, its muzzle pointed at the Kid. 'Let's have the irons, Kid,' he said. The hammer of the Winchester was eared back to full cock.

The Kid looked at Monty, but the dark of night masked his expression. Then he shrugged. 'Up to you,' he said. He pulled his rifle out by the stock and passed it to Bud. The Kid swung down from his horse, his back to Bud. He turned around with his Colt in his hand and a smile on his face. 'If I wanted, I could make you real dead, watchman.' He reversed the six-gun, jammed it in his holster, and unbuckled the gunbelt. 'Hardware's all yours,' he said, 'and it better come back without a scratch on those guns.'

'Know how to look after guns, Kid, and I got all of yours.'

'Nuff,' McCord said. 'You all're like a couple of banty roosters. Let's go see Red.'

The lookout led the way, laden with two extra rifles and two six-gun rigs. The main camp was out in the open like Red Carlisle and his bunch weren't riding herd on someone else's cows.

'Hey, Red,' Bud called. 'Monty McCord and the Kid want to talk with you.'

A tall man with broad shoulders and a narrow rider's waist stood from where he'd been sitting on an old cottonwood log. 'Monty McCord? Sumbitch.'

'Hold up.' Bud stuck his rifle across the trail to stop Monty and the Kid.

Red Carlisle stood spraddle-legged in front of the dying fire. 'Well. Whatcha waiting on? Bring 'em in. We ain't got nothing to hide.'

Monty started at that statement. *Nothing to hide.*

'Go on in,' Bud said.

'I'm coming, Red,' Monty said, his voice loud in the quiet night.

'Hey, Monty. What the hell? Ain't seen you since Llano.' Red Carlisle met Monty and the Kid with a big smile on his face. 'Them was the days, eh?'

'We was young back then, Red. Done things that don't look so good now.' Monty paused a long moment.

'Coffee?' Red said. 'Should be some in the pot. Night riders need their coffee, not that them beeves is gonna stampede off somewhere.'

'Speaking of beeves, Red, how come you to be driving a hunnert head of H Bar H cows?'

'Bought t'be paid for by a gent up Denver way,' Red said.

'Old Man Billings know what you're doing?'

'Hell, I don't know. I got a bill of sale from Barry Seagle. Said young Hartley signed him a hunnert head to pay for a poker game. Knowing Hartley, I reckon Seagle's got the right.' Red went to his saddle-bags, rummaged around, and came up with a folded sheet of paper. He held it out to Monty. 'See for yourself,' he said.

Monty took the paper and slanted it so it caught the light from the fire.

Sold to Barry Seagle
100 head of steers
branded H Bar H

Hartley Billings

The signature looked to have a bottle or two of Old Potrero behind it. Then another paragraph.

Above mentioned 100 steers are sold to Angus Maggrath for a sum to be determined upon delivery of said steers to the Maggrath slaughterhouse pens in Denver City. Same steers to be gathered and delivered by Nathaniel Carlisle and whatever crew he chooses.

Barry Seagle's signature was firm and clear.

6

Nelson Croft rode with his chin on his chest like he was thinking hard. His big bay horse had an easy gait, so it was no special effort to stay in the saddle.

'Thinking, Nels?' Monty said. 'Or sleeping?'

'Yeah,' Croft said. 'Irks the shit outta me.'

'Losing cows?'

'That, and the boss's boy signing off for a hundred head of his old man's cows.'

'Figure the old man'll fight it?' Monty's horse Baron matched the bay stride for stride. The bay seemed eager to get home. Baron went wherever Monty wanted and wasn't overly attached to any special piece of ground.

Croft opened his eyes and shot a glance at Monty, who looked straight ahead like he didn't see the look.

'You spent your spare time at Woodrow's, Monty. You tell me. You think that hunnert head was all the boy was into that cardslick for?'

'I can't rightly count the times I've heard him say to Seagle that he was good for it, what ever 'it' was.'

'Shit.'

'I reckon.'

'Damn, I hate to tell the Old Man about this. He was dead set on that boy taking over the H Bar H.'

'That'd be a sight to see.'

'It'd be OK if he'd of let me run it.'

'Wouldn't do that, eh?' Monty scrubbed a hand over the two-day stubble on his square jaw. 'You and the boy didn't get along, then?'

Croft turned to give Monty a hard stare. 'Get along? How in hell does a man get along with a shavetail boy who don't know which end of a cow the tits're on, but figures he's second cousin to God himself? No, he didn't like me, because I wouldn't put up with his stupidity around the stock, or in the pens, for that matter.'

'But the Old Man gave the boy his head?'

'He knew. Hunter Billings ain't no fool. He knew. But he couldn't let on that he did. No way he could have that boy take over the H Bar H if he let on to how stupid Hartley was. Purely stupid.'

'You can say that again.'

Croft and Monty rode several minutes without speaking. The Kid and Chunky and the H Bar H hands stayed a couple of lengths behind, letting the two men talk without interruption.

'Funny,' Croft said. 'The boy never was good with a gun. Can't remember him ever carrying one. How come he took a shot at you?'

'How in hell should I know? I was damn near out the door. I mean, I'd whacked the boy up pretty good, but I sure wasn't about to kill him. Then, while my back was turned, he took a potshot at me. Damn near tore a chunk outta my ear. There was quite a bit of smoke between me and him, but he sure as hell had a gun.'

Croft rode on, his chin on his chest, his hands one on top of the other over his saddle horn. Monty didn't say anything, he just rode alongside the H Bar H foreman, thinking thoughts of his own. Thinking about how the boy was crouched with a little Colt in his hand and fear on his battered face. Thinking how Barry Seagle was standing off to one side, a smirk on his pretty-boy face.

Barry Seagle.

'Hey Croft. You know that cardsharp Barry Seagle? The one who got the note from the boy for the hunnert head a cows?'

'Yeah.' Croft didn't move his chin from his chest.

'He was standing mighty close to the boy when I shot him. Mighty close.'

'I only got one question, McCord. What happened to the goldam gun?'

'What gun?'

'The one you said the boy shot at you with.'

'In his damn hand. He had it and I shot him. He dropped and never moved. Don't remember if he kept hold of the gun or not. Holly's yelling at me to high tail it and all.' Monty stood in his stirrups to scratch at the inside of his left thigh. He sat back with a sigh. 'I shot the boy, Croft. No two ways about it. When a man gets shot at, he naturally shoots back. To think about it, I reckon I was a little set back that Hartley had the gumption to pull a trigger at me.'

'Never come up with a gun,' Croft said. 'Yeah, Holly said Hartley shot first. He said that. But there was no gun there. Hell. I say there was no gun, but by the time we got there, they had the boy laid out on a table. No gun. No goldam gun. No way of knowing, though, for sure.'

Croft took a long look at Monty. 'Far as I know, McCord, you're a straight man. Ain't no one ever called you a liar. And the other people in Woodrow's said

Hartley took the first shot. But with what? The boy never even carried a gun.'

Monty chewed on his moustache some. He looked at the sky, and he looked at the horizon. But wherever he looked, he saw no answers. 'Were I to make a guess,' he said, 'considering that piece of paper Red Carlisle was carrying, dandyman Barry Seagle's in this fracus up to his pretty ass.'

* * *

Hunter Billings stared at the unfolded foolscap but his eyes focused on something in the far distance. He heaved a sigh, then handed the note to Ellen. 'That boy of mine sure knew how to get in trouble, but he was all I had. Now he's gone and all his troubles are mine.'

Ellen refolded the foolscap. 'You've been reaching for a lot in Twin Forks Basin,' she said. 'Maybe your reach has stretched too far.'

'I had to leave enough behind to take care of the boy,' Billings said.

'And now, even in death, he's conspiring to tear down everything you built for him.'

The face Billings turned to Ellen aged another decade as she watched.

'Don't seem to matter much any more,' Billings said. 'Hartley gone. Melinda gone. What in hell am I doing? What can be done. What makes it all worth while?'

Ellen's voice came hard and sharp. 'Hunter Billings. Don't you go blubbering and feeling sorry for yourself. You've built the biggest cattle operation in the basin and you've helped build the town my father founded. Many more people depend on you than your miserable, spoiled-rotten, gambling and carousing son.'

Billings cringed. 'It ain't nothing now. Shit. Oh. Sorry, Ellen.'

Ellen folded her arms and leaned toward Billings. 'Sell me the ranch, then,' she said. 'Sell me everything,

Hartley's debts and all.'

'Wha-a-a-at?'

'You heard me. Sell out to me. Lock, stock and barrel. Everything. You can keep this house. Live here. I'll keep your cook and get a housekeeper. And I'll bury you next to Melinda and Hartley when you're gone. Sell out to me and you get rid of all those worries. You can concentrate on getting well.'

Hunter Billings lifted his face, tilted his head back, and stared at the ceiling. Again he heaved a sigh. 'You're right. I'm in no shape to fight it out with Barry Seagle, or anyone else for that matter.'

'What's a fair price, Mr Billings?'

'How does a man put a price on his whole life?'

'I suppose you can't, but there must be some way for me to purchase your concerns.'

'What do you know of my 'concerns'?'

Ellen's lips bowed up at the corners of her mouth. 'More than you might imagine,' she said.

Billings smoothed the blankets over his legs and pulled them up around his waist. He looked everywhere but at Ellen. 'There ain't nobody left but me,' he said to the blankets. 'All I ever worked for, all I ever built, all I ever did was for Hartley, and for Melinda. Damn.'

'Damn is right,' Ellen said. 'Damn shame to let everything you built up go to ruin because your own family's gone on ahead. Dozens of people depend on your 'concerns' to make a living, Mr Billings. Would Barry Seagle do for them like you have?'

Hunter Billings raised hangdog eyes to Ellen. 'I been pretty tough on people, Ellen. Damn tough.'

'Mr Billings — '

'I wish you'd quit that Mr Billings crap. The name's Hunter. I'd rather you call me that.'

Ellen paused. Then, with her lips bowed in a smile that didn't quite reach her eyes yet, she said, 'All right, Hunter.

All right. I was about to ask you if you thought Barry Seagle would be better at looking out for the people who operate the businesses you own in Watsonville.'

'Ain't never seen that fart . . . er, 'scuse me, Ellen . . . ain't never seen him for nothing but a pretty-boy gambler.'

'Can I make a suggestion?'

'What else have you been doing all day?' Billings's smile took the sting from his words.

'It's OK, then?'

'Shoot.'

'Just what do you own in Watsonville?'

Ellen's question made Billings frown. He straightened the blankets again. 'I own Twin Forks Basin Bank,' he said, 'and the bank owns most of the businesses, and carries loans on most of the pumpkin rollers and those two little ranches over to the northeast. Not much other than the Flying W and the H Bar H that ain't in debt up to their asses.'

'How many people know you own the bank?'

Billings ran his fingers through a thatch of graying hair. 'Have to shave,' he said. 'No right to lie around with a face full of whiskers. Bad example.'

'Who knows you own the bank?'

Billings wouldn't meet Ellen's hard gaze. He put both hands to his face and scrubbed, like he was washing it with soap and water.

'Who knows, Hunter?'

'Peter Gustav, the president and acting teller. And Wilford Breckendale. Wilford runs the Lucky Lady mine. That's where I got the stake to start up the bank. The mine's about played out, though.'

'Peter, and Wilford, and . . . '

'Jimmie Clark.'

'Jimmie Clark? The Iron Skittle's Jimmie Clark?'

Billings nodded.

'Well.' Ellen could say nothing. It didn't matter how Jimmie had found out. Just that he knew. 'Anyone else?'

Billings shook his head. 'Probably not. But who knows? Does it matter?'

Ellen paced back and forth across the room, whacking her riding quirt into the palm of her left hand in time with her steps. 'Sell me the ranch, Hunter. Then sell the businesses you hold to the people who run them. They can pay the bank for the businesses a little every month, maybe — so all you have to worry about is the bank itself, and Peter would do most of the work there.'

A frown took the corners of Billings's mouth down at the corners. 'Then all I'd have is the bank?'

'How much more would you need? What are you in shape to handle? What kind of an empire do you really want now?' Ellen paused.

Billings was silent.

'Hunter Billings. Sell the H Bar H to me. Sell your interests in town. Sit back, relax, and let me fight Barry Seagle.'

Billings raised his hound-dog eyes to search Ellen's face. He took a deep breath. 'Where would I live?'

'Like I said, right here. Why should you go anywhere else?'

'You'd own the spread, though.'

'Yes, but you can live here as long as you wish.'

Billings shrank into himself, where he seemed to be holding a debate. Eventually he nodded. 'All right. I'll do it.'

'Good.' Ellen smiled. She stepped to Billings's bedside and put out her hand. 'Shake,' she said.

Billings gave her a firm handshake.

'So. You're feeling better already,' Ellen said. 'Now, let's figure out how to pay off Hartley's gambling debts.'

★ ★ ★

Monty, Chunky, the Kid, Nelson Croft, and the H Bar H cowboys rode into the ranch headquarters shortly before noon. They unsaddled their horses, rubbed them down with gunnysacks, and turned them into the remuda corral back of the barn.

'Holt, pitch some hay to them horses,' Croft said to a cowpoke, and heaved his saddle up onto the top fence rail.

'Reckon I could hit you up for a quart of oats?' Monty asked. 'Baron needs some refreshment.'

'Get it over there.' Croft waved at a plank-and-batten granary shed standing to the west of the big barn. 'Lined them grain bins with tin. Keeps the mice out so we've got more for the stock.'

Monty filled a canvas nosebag with a generous bait of oats and whistled for Baron. The sorrel came across the corral with his head high and his nostrils flared. Monty grabbed him by the mane and scratched behind his ears before letting him shove his muzzle into the nosebag. He stood at the corral fence as Baron chewed happily on H Bar H oats.

Croft came over and hooked a boot on the bottom corral pole. 'Don't like that note Red Carlisle had,' he said. 'Don't seem quite right to me.'

'Gambling ain't never right,' Monty said. 'Playing cards is OK. Throwing dice is OK. Bucking the tiger is OK. Them games is all right if you go in knowing you'll likely come out with a lot less cash.'

'You oughta know,' Croft said. 'You've spent enough time at the table there in Woodrow's.'

'Yeah, but the limit's twenty bucks. When I've lost twenty bucks, I cash out. Seagle knows that about me, and he don't like it. No way he can rope me into one of those high-stakes games. I'll sit and play as long as I've got chips on the table. When they're gone, so am I.'

'Hartley Billings didn't see it that way, I guess.' Croft frowned at the dust in the corral.

'You know, Croft, I'd be almighty surprised if that hunnert head is the only IOU young Hartley had. He was almighty full of himself, and always sure a turn of luck stood just around the corner.'

'Yeah.' Croft didn't say any more. He just stood there, digging at the dusty ground with the toe of a dusty boot.

The cookie called from the back door of the ranch house. 'Missa Croft, boss wants you, and Miss Ellen said to have Missa McCord come, too.'

'Be right there,' Croft hollered, and looked askance at Monty. 'Shit. What now?'

Monty shrugged. 'Need a couple more minutes for Baron to finish up them oats. Be in soon as he's done.'

'Well. Guess I'd better head on in. Reckon the boss's feeling up to chewing on my ears over them cows.'

'His kid done it, not you.'

'He might not see it thataway.'

'Croft, you're the best cowman in this end of the country, and I reckon Hunter Billings knows that. If he don't, I'll tell him, and if he don't listen, I'll give him another kick in the balls. If he still don't listen, we can ride for

Arizona. My friend Wolf Wilder's got a place in Lone Pine Canyon, and I hear the Hashknife Outfit's hiring.'

'I been here too long to go loping off, McCord. Twin Forks Basin is good country.'

'Y'sat here jawing so long that Baron's chawed through the oats.' Monty took the nosebag off the sorrel and hung it over a corral post, then followed Croft toward the big house.

Gerry Swift sat on the front porch with his chair leaned back against the wall. His hat was down over his eyes and a matchstick stuck out of one corner of his mouth.

'Swift,' Monty said. 'Looks quiet around.'

Swift took the matchstick from his mouth. 'Not much going on,' he said.

'Boss wants me. Any idea what for?'

Swift shrugged. 'She don't always tell me what she's thinking,' he said. 'But you'd best getchur ass in there.'

'Going, going.' Monty stepped through the door Croft held open. He stopped for a minute to take in the pine paneling and handmade furniture. 'Don't look like no rich man's house to me,' he said, half under his breath.

'Boss don't waste money,' Croft said.

'Monty. Nels.' Ellen Watson stood in the doorway to Hunter Billings's bedroom. Monty raised an eyebrow at the familiarity she showed Croft.

'Come in here,' she said. 'Mr Billings and I have things for you to do.'

Both men removed their hats and walked quietly into the room, expecting to see Hunter Billings all pale and drawn and maybe taking his last breath. But the rancher sat up in bed, pillows stuffed between his back and the headboard.

'Gentlemen,' he said. 'Miss Watson has something to say.'

'Monty. Nels. The H Bar H is now Watson property. Mr Billings has agreed to sell the ranch to me.'

'Then you'll want to know this, boss,' Monty said. 'We come on Red Carlisle and three other 'pokes a-driving a hunnert head of H Bar H cows.'

'Goldam rustler,' Billings rasped, his face turning red.

'No, sir,' Croft said. 'He had a bill of sale, signed by Hartley to Barry Seagle and then to Red Carlisle. Nothing we could do. Not a damn thing.'

Silence settled over the room. The loudest sound was Billings's breathing. Then Ellen spoke. 'Nels. You're in charge here, if you'll agree to stay. Mr Billings will live here, but you'll be in charge.'

She turned her attention to Monty as if Croft's decision was a foregone conclusion. 'We face another problem,' she said. 'Barry Seagle has more than eight thousand dollars worth of IOUs from Hartley Billings. We don't have enough cash to pay him off, but we can't have such a man taking over our town. Nels can take care of the H Bar H and Jim Blakely the Flying W. Monty, we want you to pick six cowboys, round up two thousand head of cattle, Flying W and H Bar H, and drive them to

Cheyenne. Then send back the cash to pay Seagle with.'

'Me?'

'You're the one man I'd trust,' Ellen said. 'You can do it.'

7

Monty took Chunky Willis, Aaron Tanner, Billy Bob Albert, the Kid, and two cowboys from the H Bar H, Heck Lewis and Josiah Dunkin. 'We don't want nothing under two years old,' he said, 'and they all gotta wear Flying W or H Bar H. We ain't got time to brand no mavericks.'

They rode to the eastern end of the basin and started working back. 'Take it slow,' Monty said. 'We don't wanna spook no critters into running off pounds. Slow and easy.'

The men knew how to round up cows and they knew how to separate beeves from the breeding stock. While they were starting the round-up, Monty rode over to the O Quarter Circle and the Rafter 7 spreads.

The O Quarter Circle lay in a narrow canyon that branched off the basin on the northeast corner. He rode straight in. Been years since the Utes had made any trouble and rustlers were not a problem in Twin Forks Basin . . . so far. Narrow leaf cottonwoods lined the little creek at the mouth of the canyon and meadows spread out on each side, sometimes more than a mile wide. Sage dotted the drier land that lay beyond the reach of the creek's water, and bristlecone pines grew in the rocks where the canyon walls sloped down to the meadows. Above the rocks on the round-top ridges, stands of lodgepole pine with the occasional ponderosa guarded the canyon. For a one-horse outfit, a man would have to look a long time to find a better spot. Monty felt a twinge of something that might have been envy. Some men set out to make a place for themselves. Monty McCord always rode for someone else's brand.

A woman stood before the small house and the house stood before a sheer rock face that rose at least fifty feet, mostly straight up. The only way to approach that house was from straight on. She held a '73 Winchester, hammer eared back. The gun wasn't pointed at Monty, but it wasn't out of line, either. He kept his hands on the saddle horn.

'That's close enough, mister,' the woman said.

'Orson Radley around?'

'Not so far that he can't hear this rifle go off,' she said.

Monty grinned. 'Orson's got himself a bearcat for a wife. He's a lucky man.'

The woman said nothing. The rifle edged closer to lining up on Monty's belly.

'Monty McCord's the name, ma'am. I ride for the Flying W. We're rounding up some beeves for a drive to Cheyenne and I figured as long as we're going we could take a few head of Orson's stock, too. Save you all the trouble. Whadda ya think?'

'That'd be up to Orson himself,' she said. 'But I reckon he might want to.'

'We'll bed what we've gathered at Rincon meadows tonight. You want us to take some beeves for you, have Orson ride down there to see me, could you?'

'I'll talk to him,' she said, and she stood tall and proud as one of the ponderosas on the rim above her.

'"Preciate it, Missus Radley. I'll be going along then. Got beeves to get together.' Monty lifted a forefinger to the brim of his hat, turned Baron around, and walked him back down the canyon. He wondered how much land Orson Radley held in his own name.

The Rafter 7 sat by a spring that bubbled from the ground a good mile from the foothills leading up to the Roan Plateau. It didn't have the natural protection of the Radley place, and it looked a lot more like a rawhide operation, if it was a cow outfit at all.

Hardly more than a line shack, the Rafter 7 had no stock corral, no stacks of hay for the coming winter, no pigpen, no chicken run, nothing to show it was a place where people worked a living from the land.

'Hello the house,' Monty hollered.

Silence, except for the scream of a redtailed hawk that rode a thermal off to the west.

'Hello the house,' Monty hollered again, and moved Baron closer to the weather-beaten structure. No smoke from the chimney. No animals. No sign of human occupation. Monty dismounted and pulled his Winchester from the saddle boot. He jacked a shell into the chamber.

'Hello the house,' he hollered once more.

Still no answer.

The door had a piggin string through a hole so someone outside could pull up the bar inside. Monty pulled the string and the door swung into the room. A miasma of stale air, rot, and musty odors issued from the house.

'I'm coming in,' Monty said, speaking loud enough to be heard throughout the house. He thumbed back the Winchester's hammer and let the rifle muzzle precede him into the house.

The dust on the table, the grit on the floor, and the dead silence inside the house seemed to say no one was home, and that no one had been there for days, maybe weeks. Where was Ben Stacey, then? Monty had seen him only once in Watsonville, what, six months ago? 'Ben? Ben Stacey?' Monty stood with his head cocked, listening.

Was it the wind rustling? A whisper? Monty moved carefully across the room toward the single doorway in the back wall. An old cavalry blanket hung from the head of the doorframe to separate the back room from the living area. Monty leaned the Winchester beside the door and carefully pulled his Colt from its holster at his right buttock. Pistols are quicker to use in close quarters, and he used the barrel to shove the blanket to one side.

It might have been a moan, but the sound was too low for Monty to be sure. The room was too dark for him to see anything right away. The smell of shit and piss and who knows what made Monty's eyes water.

The tiny moan came again. This time Monty realized it issued from a mound of ragged bedclothes on an old four-poster that might once have been in some uppity back-East house.

The mound moved. Just barely, but it moved. A hand came out, slowly reaching with fingers like twigs on a sapling.

Monty eared back the Colt's hammer. He didn't know if lead could down ghosts, but there'd be no harm in trying.

'H . . . H . . . H . . . He . . . lp. He . . . lp . . . me,' the mound of rags said. The whisper sounded like a dry wind rustling through the bare limbs of an old cottonwood tree. Dry and raspy.

Monty shifted the Colt to his left hand. He couldn't shoot as well with his left, but six feet away, all a man had to do was point the gun and pull the trigger. Usually the bullet found something to hit.

He stepped carefully toward the foul-smelling mound. The hand dropped and lay unmoving atop the bedclothes.

Monty slithered to the head of the four-poster and gingerly moved the top blanket. A head appeared, shrunken almost beyond recognition, with the skin like paper against the bone. The eyes sank deep into the skull, and they were open. In them, Monty could see a spark, a deep desire to live, a will that would not break. 'Hang on there, Ben. Just you hold on.'

'Wa . . . wa . . . ter.' The sound was almost a sigh. It came from a mouth with thin lips drawn back to show old ivory teeth. Cracks in the lips showed little black droplets of blood. The sunken eyes looked at Monty as if he were the Savior.

'Hang on, Ben,' Monty said again. He holstered the Colt and ran for the canteen hanging on Baron's saddle.

Little dust devils stirred up by Monty's passing settled back to the floor as he plunged into the gloom of the bedroom, canteen in hand. He threw back the bedclothes covering Ben Stacey and nearly gagged at the stench. But this was no time for pussyfooting. Monty clamped his jaws and breathed through clenched teeth. Ben Stacey's stick-like arm and twiggy fingers reached for the canteen. Sunk deep into their sockets, his eyes saw only the canteen and its promise of water.

'Ah . . . ah . . . ah.' Each breath Stacey took seemed to plead for moisture.

Monty tipped a drop or two of water from the canteen into Stacey's gaping mouth.

The emaciated man gargled and wheezed, but the water went down.

'Ah . . . ah . . . ah.' Stick fingers scrabbled at the canteen.

'Not too fast, Ben. Take it easy. I got the water. You just lie back and drink it down.' Monty dribbled a few drops into

Stacey's maw. This time, it went down easier.

Monty took the better part of an hour to feed most of a canteen full of water to Stacey, who lay under a mound of foul bedcothes — an old army blanket, a quilt some woman had lovingly stitched in the distant past, a comforter with cotton batting sticking out of holes in the cover. What were once clean muslin sheets now showed the watermarks of old urine and the foul smell told Monty that Ben had not been strong enough to get out of bed to shit.

Ben Stacey lay back, his breathing still labored.

'Ben. You hear me?'

Stacey's nod was just a tiny movement of his head.

'I'm gonna leave, Ben.'

Stacey's eyes flew open. His hand clamped on Monty's forearm with surprising strength. 'Ah! Ah!'

'Ben, it's me, Monty McCord. You never seen the day I'd tell you a lie. I'm going, Ben, because you need more help than I can give you. I'll fill up the canteen before I go. Someone will come for you with a wagon. I promise.'

Monty looked down at the skeleton of a man. 'I don't know who done what to you, Ben, but you'd better not die on me. I'll be back to help you get what's yours.'

He looked into Ben Stacey's eyes for a long time, and at last Stacey nodded his agreement and let go of Monty's arm.

'Somebody will be here to help you soon,' Monty said. He took the canteen and refilled it at the spring. 'Hang in there, Ben,' he said as he placed the canteen within easy reach. But Ben Stacey didn't answer. Only the very slow movement of his chest said he was still alive.

Monty rode Baron away at a long lope. He found the gather at Seven Mile tank and sent the Kid to the H Bar H with news of Stacey's predicament.

They'd rounded up about 1,500

head by the time a wagon came from the H Bar H. Nelson Croft held the reins and Ellen Watson sat beside him on the high seat — much too close to Monty's way of thinking, but Ellen was the boss and Monty had no claim on her. Besides, Nelson Croft was as good a cowman as there was in Twin Forks Basin.

'Y'all know where Ben Stacey's Rafter 7 is?' Monty fixed his eyes on Ellen, ignoring Croft.

'I know,' Ellen said. 'Is he as bad as Elroy described?'

'Elroy?'

'Yes, Monty. The Kid has a name. Elroy Daws.'

'No shit. Er, sorry, boss. Elroy Daws, eh? Any relation to Sudden Daws?'

'Jake Daws? Yes. Jake Daws, the man called Sudden, is Elroy's father.'

'I'll be damned. No wonder he's slick with a gun. Sudden's his pa. Ha!'

'The gather looks good, Monty,' Croft said.

'I reckon we'll have a couple of

thousand in two or three days,' Monty said. He toed the ground with his boot, then spoke again to Ellen. 'Boss, there don't seem to be as many cows on the range as people think, ours or theirs.' He jerked his head toward Croft.

'I trust you to give me an accurate assessment when this is all over, Monty. But right now, we need the money from a drive to Cheyenne, and Ben Stacey needs help.' Ellen spoke to Croft. 'Nels, let's go help that poor man.'

Monty watched the light wagon roll away. The boss would take care of Ben. He turned his attention to the gather and the way to Cheyenne, Wyoming Territory.

* * *

The herd seemed content at being held in Buford's Meadow, about three miles north of Flying W headquarters. Monty wondered what had happened to Ben Stacey, but getting ready for the drive to Cheyenne took all his time and

115

attention. Besides, if the herd was to beat the snow over South Pass, they needed to be on their way.

Cinch McDougal showed up with his chuck wagon full of pinto beans and onions and rice and flour and sourdough starter. 'The beeves look good,' he said to Monty. 'Reckon you've got a head or two extry for us to chaw on the trail.'

'I reckon. Can't make a drive without losing a few and gaining a few. Slow elk won't make all that much difference. You bring bullets?'

'Not all that many. Four boxes of .45s, four of .44–40s, and a box of .45–70s for my Springfield. Oh, and some 10-gauge shotgun shells.'

'Too bad you didn't bring a 410. You coulda plinked a few prairie chickens or grouse or pigeons or something. Beef and SOB stew gets awful tiresome on the trail.' Monty's smile took the sting from his words.

'Get outta here,' Cinch said. 'I gotta get dinner going.'

Gabriel Baca wrangled the remuda in. Every drover would need extra mounts, four or five, probably, and Gabe had to keep them up with the herd.

The day before the drive started Ellen Watson and Nelson Croft rode into Buford's Meadow with Deerstone not far behind. They dismounted near the cook fire and Cinch got them all cups of coffee.

'How's Ben?' Monty asked. 'How'd he ever get into a mess like that?'

'Ben's recovering, Monty. We still don't know all that happened to him. His memory's a bit spotty,' Ellen said.

'Damn.' Monty spat. 'No man should have to go through something like that.'

'No, but don't worry about it now. You've a herd to get to Cheyenne.'

'That I do.'

'Deerstone will go along to scout the way for you. His people know these hills best.'

'Cheyenne's Arapaho country.'

Ellen's eyes smiled. 'So he says. But

he'll see you through. And Monty, we need the proceeds from the cattle sale in ninety days.'

'Ninety days?'

'Counting today. You can have Wells Fargo in Cheyenne wire the money to Wells Fargo in Denver.'

'Shit. 'Scuse me, boss.'

'Deerstone says he knows ways to shorten the drive. Let's hope he's right.'

'He prolly knows,' Monty said. 'A man can plan on fifteen miles a day and then the critters stampede and it takes three days to gather them up again, if you ain't lost no cowboys.' Monty scowled and stomped at a stink bug making its way toward a nearby cow pie.

'Eight hunnert miles, give or take. Figure twelve miles a day . . . so if things go right, which they rarely do, we'll be there by early September. Shouldn't be snowing yet, and the critters'll have some grass along the way.' Monty heaved a sigh. 'Best be on our way, then.'

'I'm . . . we're counting on you, Monty McCord. The H Bar H and the Flying W are in your hands. God be with you,' Ellen said.

Monty turned his attention to Nelson Croft. 'You're as good a cowman as there is in this country, Croft, but'f you don't treat my boss right, you'll have me and Jim Blakely and the rest of the Flying W hands riding roughshod over your dead body. You hear me?'

For a moment, Croft looked upset. Then he relaxed. 'El means as much to me as she does to you all. Rest easy, Monty, and get those cows to Cheyenne. El trusts you. I trust you.'

Croft thrust out a hand in Monty's direction. Monty took a step forward and gripped it. 'You take care of the boss, I'll take care of the cows,' he said.

8

Barry Seagle dealt cards at Woodrow's saloon with a smug look on his face. He'd allowed the Flying W and the H Bar H three months, ninety days, to pay off Hartley Billings's debts in cash, or forfeit the ranches. And forfeit of the ranches would naturally give him control of Watsonville. Once the town was his, he'd get the name changed. Seagleton had a much more sophisticated ring to it than Watsonville.

The batwing doors opened and Seagle looked to see what new fodder for his game had entered.

A tall black silhouette stood in the open doorway, and Seagle's eyes sparked with anticipation. Chico Valdez. The man Seagle wanted to stymie the cattle drive to Wyoming. If no cattle got to Cheyenne, no money would be available to redeem the bumpkin's IOUs.

'Chico,' Seagle called. 'Over here.'

The gunman released the batwings he'd held open and strode across the sawdust-strewn floor. He came to a halt in front of Seagle's table.

'Hello, Chico,' Seagle said.

The Mexican gunman nodded. '*¿Qué tal?*' he said.

Seagle shrugged. Chico Valdez hadn't changed since El Paso. His face was still hard. He still wore a short-brimmed black hat. His shirt and trousers were still black, though grayed with trail dust. His pistols gleamed, the tools of a gunman. One rested in a right-hand holster of a normal gun rig, the other rode high on his left hip, the handle slanted forward for a quick cross draw. Both were nickel-plated Colt SAA in .45 caliber.

'I rode all the way from El Paso del Norte, *gringo*,' Chico said. 'Whatever is happening had better be good — *obligatorio que sera muy bueno.*'

Seagle showed his dealer's smile, teeth sparkling — he brushed them every day. 'Of course. Of course. Give me a minute.'

He gathered up the cards. 'Gentlemen,' he said to the drummer and the miner who sat at his table. 'The game is closed for the moment. I have some business to conduct with this gentleman. You may cash out if you wish, or you may have a drink and wait for me to return.'

'You footin' the drinks?' the miner asked.

Seagle's dealer smile stayed in place. 'Naturally,' he said. 'Holly,' he called, 'A drink for these gentlemen, and my bottle please.'

The bartender scurried over with a whiskey bottle that was half full. He had two glasses in the other hand. 'Yer Turley's Mill, Barry,' he said. 'Where you want I should put it?'

Seagle stood and took the bottle and the glasses. 'Which room upstairs is free?'

'Ain't no one in thirteen since Jenny left,' Holly said.

'Thirteen it is, then.' Seagle held no superstition concerning numbers. He'd been a gambler for too long to believe there was any such thing as Lady Luck.

'No Cuervo?' Chico said.

'This is Colorado, Chico. Tequila is not the drink of choice. You'll have to settle for good whiskey.'

'Beer,' Chico said.

'Holly, a beer to room thirteen.'

'Gotcha, Barry.'

'Follow me,' Seagle said. He mounted the stairs and went to Room 13 with Chico Valdez a step behind.

The room had a bed and a chair and a commode table. No bedclothes. No washbasin. Nothing to indicate a whore had recently plied her trade there.

'Bed or chair?' Seagle said.

Chico sat in the chair.

A rap on the door, then Holly barged in with a tall glass of beer. 'Here ya go,' he said with bartender's bonhomie.

Chico took the glass. '*Gracias*,' he

said. He waited until the sound of the bartender's footsteps faded. 'What is it, Seagle? *¿Que pasa?*'

'There's a herd gathered about ten miles northwest of town. They're planning to drive the beasts to Wyoming. I don't want them to succeed.'

'That's all?'

'Take the cattle if you can, but, by any means, stop the drive.'

'That kind of *trabajo* is not without cost.'

Seagle fished a small leather sack from inside his vest. 'This should help,' he said. He handed the poke to Chico, who opened the drawstring.

'Gold dust?'

'That's all a certain gent had with which to pay his gambling debts,' Seagle said. 'Feels to me like about a pound and a half. I reckon it'll be eight hundred dollars or so.'

Chico gave Seagle a gunman's smile. He pocketed the gold. 'A down payment,' he said. 'A *small* down payment. You ask me to do a very large job. This gold will buy you a few men. If they are good enough, I will take the animals. One day, I will return, and you will pay three times the down payment. Or you will die.'

Seagle's dealer smile never left his face, but a cold chill swept through his guts. All or nothing. That's what it came down to. All or nothing. And Seagle wanted all.

'Triple the down payment when and if you return,' Seagle said, 'but if you can take the cows, they can be sold at Uncompahgre Agency.'

'How many cows?'

'I'm told more than two thousand. Forty thousand dollars at twenty a head. Your share is one fourth. Agreed?'

'Sí, aprobado.' Chico sipped his beer, then spat it on the floor. '¡Carajo! No tequila. No good beer. No beautiful señoritas. I shall be happy to return to El Paso del Norte.' He stood, put the nearly full glass of beer on the commode table, and left. No handshake.

125

* ★ ★

Monty moved the herd off Buford's Meadow shortly after dawn. Deerstone had left during the night.

Billy Bob Albert took the point, with Chunky Willis and Heck Lewis riding swing with Aaron Tanner and Josiah Dunkin. Kent Radley and the Kid rode drag. Radley had sent fifty-seven steers and his boy to go with the gather. Kent rode drag to gain experience and the Kid to keep an eye on their back trail. Gabriel Baca cared for the remuda.

An old brindle cow took the lead like it was her natural right and the herd of two- and three-year-olds followed her like she was their own mammy. Monty'd had her cut out of the gather at least a dozen times, but every morning she was back amidst the youngsters and always stepped out in the lead, seeming to understand where the drovers wanted her to go even before they'd set the direction. She set a good pace, too, head down, long curved horns pointing up the trail, and the worn tassel of her tail swishing across her haunches.

When the gather stopped at Buford's Meadows, Billy Bob came up beside Baron on the steeldust he liked so well. 'Monty, that old brindle's worth her weight in silver dollars,' he said. 'She loves to head out, she knows which way to go, and she gets the steers to follow. Saves a lotta chousing on the flanks. I vote we let her stay, even if we gotta give her away in Cheyenne.'

Monty gave Billy Bob's suggestion at least three seconds' worth of thought. 'We'll eat her if she don't keep up,' he said.

'She'll last longer than that big sorrel horse you ride,' Billy Bob said with a grin. 'I'll bet a month's wages on it.'

'You got a bet,' Monty said, sticking out a hand.

Billy Bob shook, betting on the old brindle cow. Now he rode point and the old brindle took the way he showed her.

The herd went through Roscoe Gap and found Deerstone waiting. He waved at Billy Bob and led the way to a ford on the Gunnison River. He'd already shown Cinch the way, and the chuck wagon was unlimbered, the dutch ovens were on the fire, and hot coffee awaited. A swale in the flat country between the Gunnison and the Grand rivers gave the herd a good place to graze and bed down.

Then, as Monty was assigning watches, a group of Ute braves came riding from the south. Deerstone walked out to greet them. He met the warriors about fifty yards from the cook fire. They were not a war party. No feathered war bonnets or painted faces. Monty got Baron from the picket line and rode out to see what the Utes wanted.

'I think it's a good deal,' Deerstone said as Monty approached.

'What is?'

'Paatangwaci and his men will watch our drive, tell us if strangers come.'

'Why would they do something like that?'

'I am Ute. These Uncompahgre are my brothers.'

'My brother doesn't give a tinker's damn about me,' Monty said.

Deerstone put on a smile. 'White man,' he said.

'So what do they want?'

'Meat.'

'Meat?'

'Two cows,' Deerstone said.

Monty chewed on his upper lip for a moment. Cheyenne lay 800 miles north and east. Extra lookouts couldn't hurt, and they'd pick up more than two strays on the way. 'Done,' he said. 'Who's the leader?'

Deerstone spoke to the man in front of the warriors.

He nodded and kneed his pony over to face Monty. 'I am Paatangwaci,' he said. 'My brother says Monty McCord has only one tongue and it talks straight.'

'That's true,' Monty said. 'I speak

straight to my friends. Deerstone is my friend. He says Paatangwaci is his brother, so you are my friend.'

'That is good.'

'I will have three steers cut out for you.'

Deerstone's eyes widened for an instant.

'Friends,' Monty said to him.

Deerstone agreed. 'Friends,' he said.

The cowboys had gathered by the fire and sat on their horses, watching the Indians. Monty hollered at them. 'Hey, Kid.'

The Kid loped his remuda brown over to Monty. He looked askance at the Ute warriors. He sidled the horse so it stood between Monty and the Indians. 'Whadda ya need, boss?' The Kid had taken to calling Monty 'boss' since the drive started.

'Get the boy and cut out three laggards from the herd, then give them to the Utes.'

'Our beeves? To them . . . them . . . Redskins?'

'You listen to me,' Monty said. 'You may be plenty glad you did later on.'

'Yo,' the Kid said, and reined the brown back toward the herd. He motioned the Radley boy over, had a word with him, then rode toward the browsing herd. Monty could see they were looking for specific steers. Deerstone and Paatangwaci talked in quiet tones, watching the Kid and the Radley boy cut out three critters. One limped slightly on its offside foreleg. One had a broken horn that was deformed and twisted around until it threatened to puncture the steer's eye. The third was a thick-bodied brute of a steer with abnormally short legs.

'Paatangwaci,' Monty said. 'These beeves can't keep up with their brothers. They are yours.'

The Ute raised his hand to Monty, and rode to his band. Two warriors split off and took over driving the animals. The Kid didn't look pleased and his hand never strayed far from his gun.

'Kid.'

131

He rode the brown over to Monty and Deerstone.

'Kid. You're as good a trail watcher as there is. But I'm thinking there's people who don't want these beeves to get to Cheyenne. Maybe a bunch of people. Them Utes'll keep an eye out from here to South Pass. You may never see 'em. That's OK. But if one comes running in, don't wait to see what he's got to say, you just get to me quick as you can. Hear?'

'Gotcha,' the Kid said, never taking his eyes off the Indians.

'You got something against Injuns, Kid?'

'Utes killed my ma's folks in the Meeker War,' he said.

Monty could think of nothing to say. The Kid kept watching the Indians, right hand near his gun. A young brave stopped his pony and stared back at the Kid. The air between them fairly crackled. Paatangwaci said something to the youngster. He kneed his pony after the three beeves, watching the Kid as long as he could.

'Badger Son,' Deerstone said. 'Blue-coats killed his father at Mill Creek. He has no love for white men.'

The Kid gave Deerstone a startled glance. 'Shee-it,' he said.

'Watch your mouth,' Monty said.

'Shit.' The Kid reined the brown toward the chuck wagon, turning his back to the Indians. He never looked at them again.

Monty watched the Kid go. He'd had to grow up faster than a boy should have to, and his skills with a gun and a knife sometimes exceeded his experience in life. Still, he was a good man and one who hated unfairness; Monty figured he'd just found out that Indians got the rough end of the stick just like whites. Be interesting to see how the new realization affected the Kid.

Baron went back on the picket line. He'd earned a rest and Monty would ride a lineback dun from the remuda when he started out the following morning. Right now, after Baron's quick rubdown, he aimed to get a plate of whatever slumgullion Cinch had thrown together and grab a good hot cup of coffee. He went through his plate of beans and biscuits like a coyote through a flock of chickens. The plate went into the dirty dish tub, and Monty sat back on his heels with a big tin cup of strong black coffee to help him size up the situation.

One day into a drive, herding two thousand longhorns over a trail that might not even exist. One day. That's all he could do. Move the critters north one day at a time.

Monty sipped at the coffee. 'Damn it, Cinch. A feller would think you could make a decent cup of coffee after all the years you been doing it.'

'Shutchur mouth, boss. That's as good as any coffee you're likely to get on the trail, 'n' better'n most.' Cinch's shout carried a hint of laughter. 'Y'all know coffee ain't no good lessen it puts hair on your chest. You're slurpin' down the best Ol' Arbuckles' got to offer.'

Monty kept a serious face, but inside he grinned. Cinch knew how to feed a trail crew and his coffee was downright tasty. He sucked in a mouthful, held it for a moment, then swallowed. It felt like the coffee coated his innards with a layer of whang leather. Off to the south, lightning flickered, then thunder grumbled.

9

Monty doubled the night riders in case the storm down over the San Juans moved north in the night. Spits of lightning lit the horizon to the south and thunder rumbled as a faint echo of the twickering light. Not enough wind to notice, but who knew what was pushing the clouds northward. He'd switched his saddle to the lineback and had the horse tethered close at hand. He poured some coffee into his tin cup, gulped at it, and spat the mouthful out on the ground.

'Hey, Cinch. Can't you even keep a goldam cup of coffee hot?'

Cinch came around the chuck wagon, wiping his hands on his apron. 'You want sourdough biscuits in the morning, you're gonna have to take your spurs outta my flanks and climb down off my back. How many times you been down the trail, Monty? I figure enough so's you can tell whether a cup of Arbuckle's is steaming or not.'

Monty frowned. 'Thinking, Cinch. I was thinking.'

The cook moved the coffee pot up against the coals left from the cooking fire. 'Give 'er a minute or two while you think. It'll be hot enough.'

'Yeah, I reckon.' Monty's flash of grumpiness was gone. 'Whadda you think, Cinch?' He waved at the southern skyline. Flickers still outlined the hills and grumbles of thunder still came, but a bit louder, it seemed.

Four men circled the herd, singing in low gentle voices. Usually two were enough. The sky was silent now, but clouds still rolled north. They cut off the moonlight and turned the summer night into a muggy pit of muffled sounds that seemed to carry the threat of death.

Just after midnight, a jagged bolt of lightning severed the darkness. A thunderclap destroyed the silence and overpowered the soothing cowboy songs. Monty McCord and the sleeping longhorns leaped to their feet in the same instant. Monty jumped aboard the lineback remuda horse he'd tethered within reach. The steers surged north like they'd already had a meeting and decided which direction to go if lightning ever struck.

The chuck wagon stood west and a little south of where the herd had bedded down, and at the moment was in no danger of being stomped into splinters by stampeding steers. Cinch had already gathered implements and tossed them into the wagon. 'Get outta here,' he shouted to Monty. 'I'll manage.'

Monty touched the lineback with his spurs and the horse leaped after the thundering steers. A good horse is faster than any cow and the lineback showed he was a good horse.

For a moment, Deerstone rode beside Monty. 'Cliffs ahead,' he shouted. 'Maybe two, three miles. Only one way down.'

He slapped the reins to his paint horse and the pony left Monty and the lineback like they were at a trot.

Monty pulled the thong off the hammer of his six-gun and brought the weapon up, pointed straight overhead. He fired three fast shots and, filling his lungs with air and dust, he roared, 'Mill 'em east. Turn 'em with the clock!'

The lineback raced along the west side of the wild-eyed herd. On a hogback to Monty's left a pine tree crackled and burned, victim of the lightning strike.

The herd ran.

The cowboys gathered on the west edge of the undulating mass of cattle. They had to shout, and even then only a few words.

'Billy Bob. Chunky. Get the leaders turned. Cliff up ahead,' Monty shouted.

The riders gigged their mounts and headed for the lead steers at a dead run.

'All right. Line the west side. Push 'em east. East!'

The Kid dropped back with the Radley boy to push at the tail end of the stampede. The others strung out against the flank of the beast that was a couple of thousand maddened steers.

Monty spurred the lineback after Billy Bob and Chunky. The steers out front had to be turned. The herd had to be milled. They had to be, or they'd rimrock themselves, and the boss wouldn't get the cash she needed.

The brindle cow ran in the lead, head held high, seven-foot horns swinging. Billy Bob took the chance. He urged his little Texas pony up against the brindle cow, watching the horns. He swung his looped lariat against the side of her head. She flinched and edged a little east. He whacked her again, and she turned further.

Monty and Chunky waved coiled lariats and shouted and pushed at the steers that followed the brindle cow like she was magnetized. They turned a little with the cow.

Then the brindle decided she didn't

want anything to do with the rider smacking her face with a stinging lariat. For the first time since the lightning had struck, she bawled. She headed east, and the steers followed.

Billy Bob's horse hit some kind of hole and went down. The cowboy shook his feet from the stirrups and hit the ground running straight south toward the cliff. Monty worked his horse in between the stampeding steers and the sprinting cowboy. He kept the herd turning. 'Mill 'em. Mill 'em,' he roared.

The cowboys pushed at the herd, but the steers didn't want to turn. The mass of cattle broadened as they thundered east, and soon the herd was scattered across a mile of Colorado highland. The old brindle cow maintained her speed, outdistancing her followers. They lost sight of their leader, became confused, forgot whatever it was that got them to run, slowed to a fast trot, and then a slow one. They took to the washes and the piñons and the scrub oaks. They wouldn't go far, but they'd be hell to gather come daylight.

Cinch set up the chuck wagon at the edge of the cliff above the Grand River. He had a fire and hot coffee. Billy Bob already had another horse from the remuda, a blood bay with black stockings and mane.

'Got those beeves turned just in time, boss. Little more northward and they'd of trampled me into little pieces.'

Monty waved a hand. 'Goes with the job,' he said. 'Horse?'

'Don't look like his leg's broke. He'll limp a while, I reckon, then come around.'

'Can he keep up?'

'Boss, we're gonna spend all day rounding them steers up. Shit. He'll have a full day off, maybe more. Then we gotta cross the Grand.'

'You keep your eye on him, Billy Bob. Gabriel will too, but he's your mount.'

'Will do.' Billy Bob tossed his coffee dregs into the fire. 'Funny about that lightning,' he said. 'Big bang. No rain. Something to be glad about. Hate to have to round up those critters while it's raining.'

'Rain or shine, we've got it to do. Amble down the north side of these cows and see if you can't find Old Brindle. I figure she'll mark the east end of the herd.'

'Seen Chunky?' Billy Bob asked.

'He'll be around,' Monty said. 'You go on ahead to the east. I'll catch up.'

'Yeah.' Billy Bob rinsed his cup and put it in his saddle-bags. He climbed aboard the bay and waved a hand at Monty. 'Be back in time for breakfast,' he said, 'or maybe dinner.' He gigged the bay up the cliff line.

Monty finished his own cup of coffee. The cowboys drifted in, drank Cinch's mud, and struck out to gather the scattered steers. The cook kept the coffee pot hot and brewed more coffee the moment it was empty.

The day dawned overcast, but without even a drizzle. Monty rode to the east end of the herd, cut south, and turned steers north whenever he found any brushed up and hiding. He could hear the cowboys hollering at the cows and unconsciously identified the voices. Billy Bob. Chunky. Aaron. Heck. The Kid. Kent.

He'd just shooed a big black steer out from a stand of juniper when the Kid came busting over a rise to the west like the whole Apache nation was on his tail. He sawed his little gray gelding to a stiff-legged stop almost stirrup to stirrup with Monty.

'What's the all-fired hurry, Kid?'

'Boss, you gotta come see.'

'What I gotta do is get these critters over to where the rest of the herd is.'

'Come on. You gotta see.'

Grumbling, Monty reined the lineback after the Kid's gray. The Kid kept the gelding at a slow trot, so Monty soon rode alongside.

'What's up?' Monty asked.

The Kid grinned.

'Shit,' Monty said.

They topped the rise to look down on a little swale that formed a bit of a meadow. Nearly a hundred steers were there, most content to crop at the foxtail grass. Then Monty took a second look. More steers filtered through the jack pines across the swale as if pushed by the southerly breeze, which brought with it the scent of warm beeves, fresh manure, and something else. Something akin to what a man smells when he rides into an Indian camp. Wet buckskin? Smoked jerky? Stale piss? It wasn't that a cowboy smelled any less fragrant, just different.

After the steers came the Utes.

'Them Redskins've been scaring our cows outta the brush and back to where we can hold 'em,' the Kid said. 'How 'bout that?'

Monty showed a ghost of a smile. 'Reckon them three beeves we given 'em are repaid a couple of times over, eh?'

'Yoooo weee,' the Kid said, and spurred his gray around the edge of the clearing toward the Utes. Monty followed, keeping the lineback to an easy lope.

The last of the steers cleared the trees and ambled out into the swale, eager to get their share of the rich foxtail grass. The Utes stopped at the tree line. The Kid kept his horse going pell-mell toward the Indians. Maybe he knew what would happen, maybe not.

As the Kid neared, Badger Son broke from the Utes. Paatangwaci shouted after him, but the youngster had eyes only for the oncoming cowboy.

'Kid!' Monty hollered, but the youngster paid no more attention to him than Badger Son did to Paatangwaci. It looked like the young riders were going to run their horses straight into each other.

A dozen yards from collision, the Kid pulled up, putting the gray into a stiff-legged, haunches down, sliding stop. Badger Son did the same, and the Kid's gray stood cheek by jowl with Badger Son's paint. The Kid's hand strayed toward the six-shooter at his hip. His left held the reins, pulling the gray around in a tight circle. Badger Son's right hand was on the handle of a long knife shoved into a sheath at his waist. He guided the paint with his knees, matching the Kid's gray as it turned.

Two times around in a tight circle the cowboy and the Indian rode, then the Kid stopped. Monty pulled the line-back up a couple of yards short of the youngsters. He was about to say something when the Kid moved. Staring straight into the eyes of Badger Son, he slowly raised his right hand, fingers slightly apart.

'I hear your mom got killed by bluecoat soldiers,' he said. 'My mother's mom and dad got killed by Utes in the Meeker War. I know how you feel.'

'One cannot know,' Badger Son growled. Somewhere he'd learned English.

'I know,' the Kid said, his hand stilled raised.

'Kid,' Monty said.

'Let them be, boss.' Deerstone walked his horse up alongside Monty's and stopped. Monty chastised himself for not being aware of Deerstone. A slip-up like that could get a man killed.

'I want to borrow your knife,' the Kid said. 'Please.'

Monty had never heard the Kid say *please* before. He sat the lineback, his eyes fixed on the Kid, his hands placed on top of his saddle horn.

Badger Son stared at the Kid long and hard. Then he reversed the knife and offered it handle first.

The Kid took it.

Their ponies stood nose to tail, content to rest while their riders palavered.

The Kid dallied the gray's reins around the saddle horn. He tested the knife edge with his thumb and gave a little nod. He opened his left hand, palm up, and cut it with Badger Son's knife. Blood welled.

Badger Son's eyes widened as the Kid returned the knife, handle first, then held out his bleeding hand, palm up, his eyes on Badger Son's face.

Monty sat easy on the lineback. He caught a flash of blue in the jack pines as a jay flitted from tree to tree. The clouds seemed to lower, closing in on the mountain meadow.

After a long moment, Badger Son nodded. He sliced into his own left palm and grasped the Kid's hand, mixing blood with blood. 'We who have lost,' he said, 'join our blood so we will not lose again. Thus shall it be, for ever.'

'Amen,' the Kid said. He let go of Badger Son's hand and turned the gray toward the steers in the swale. 'Come on,' he said to Monty. 'Ain't got all day.'

'You go ahead,' Monty said. 'I'll have a word with Paatangwaci.' He and Deerstone walked their horses toward the Utes.

'Hey, Badger Son,' the Kid yelled. He reined the gray back to the Indian's paint. He dug into his offside saddle-bag and brought out a Colt

Peacemaker. He handed it to Badger Son, then dug out a box of cartridges, which he gave to the Ute as well. 'Protect yourself and yours when you must,' he said. 'Brother.'

He turned the gray and once again rode toward the steers. As he started them moving toward the gathering place, Badger Son let out a whoop. Holding the Peacemaker above his head, he danced the paint around in a circle, then walked the pony back to where the rest of the Utes waited. He handed the pistol to Paatangwaci, who turned it over in his hands, half-cocked the hammer, and spun the cylinder. He nodded and gave the gun back to Badger Son.

'Paatangwaci,' Monty hollered. 'Hold up a bit.' He gigged the lineback into a trot. Deerstone rode a half-length behind. Four or five yards from the Utes, the lineback stopped of its own accord.

Monty sat silent for a moment. 'We thank the Uncompahgre for bringing out cattle,' he said. 'Do your people hunger?'

'We had three cows,' Paatangwaci said. 'We have two now.'

'Last night, our cows stampeded,' Monty said. 'I think we cannot find them all.' He pulled his tally book from his vest pocket along with a pencil stub. He licked the point of the pencil and wrote:

Paatangwaci of the Ute tribe and his people have permission to hunt and take any Flying W cattle strays in the area south of the Grand River.

He signed the note Monty McCord, trail boss, and handed it to Paatangwaci. 'Any cows you find after we have crossed the Grand are yours for your people,' he said. 'If anyone tries to stop you, show them that paper.'

Paatangwaci took the torn tally-book page. 'We know of papers,' he said. 'Those we put our marks on yesterday have little meaning today.'

'I hear you,' Monty said. 'I can only vouch for myself. As long as I work for the Flying W brand, that paper says it all. The strays are yours.' He started to rein the lineback around, then stopped. 'Just make sure the strays have Flying W brands,' he said.

Deerstone said something in the Ute tongue. Monty waited until he'd finished. 'Let's run them steers over to the main herd.' He gigged the lineback into a lope.

The Kid already had the steers headed north, so Monty and Deerstone took positions on either flank.

'Hyah. Hyah,' the Kid hollered and slapped his chaps with a coiled lariat.

'Hyah there,' Monty echoed.

Deerstone rode silent.

The steers gave them no trouble. Just before he rode into the trees bordering the meadow, the Kid reined in his gray and turned to look back across the swale. The Utes were gone except for Badger Son, who sat astride his paint at the edge of the jack pines on the meadow's southern border.

'Wai-ha-ee-oh,' Badger Son screeched. He held the Peacemaker high above his head. 'My brother,' he shouted. 'Take care!'

The Kid doffed his hat and waved it. 'See ya when I get back, brother,' he shouted, and plunged the gray into the trees.

The clouds began to drizzle.

10

The Flying W and H Bar H riders bunched the herd at the edge of the canyon rim, close to a wash that would allow the cattle to get down to the banks of the Grand. They did a fast tally and found they'd lost just over twenty head. The only casualty among the drovers was Billy Bob's horse, which seemed to have sprained its leg, and the Kid's cut hand.

With the steers up against the edge of the canyon, half the drovers could take off to have coffee, biscuits and sowbelly at the chuck wagon. Cinch had it parked west of the herd. He'd stretched a tarp out front over the wagon, poled up at the ends, and built a place where off-duty cowboys could get out of the drizzling rain.

'Dumb shit,' Cinch said to the Kid. 'Dumb ass. That's all I got to say.' He wiped the Kid's palm with a finger dipped in lard, then bound the wound with a strip of cloth cut from a flour sack. 'Now get outta here.'

The Kid grinned. 'Ain't ever'day a man gets to be blood brother to an Injun. May come in handy some time.'

'You're head's so far up your own ass you wouldn't know 'handy' if it bit you.' Cinch snorted. 'Eatchur goldam food. Shee-it.'

The Kid ducked his head and chomped off a big chunk of sourdough and sowbelly. He chewed dutifully, but couldn't get the smile off his face.

'Shove them vittles down your face and go relieve Heck. Let him get a cup of mud.' Monty's voice was stern but his face told the Kid he'd done well.

'Gotcha, boss.' The Kid gobbled the remainder of his biscuit and bacon, washed it down with the lukewarm coffee in his cup, and tossed the cup in the dishpan. 'I'll come back for the cup,' he said.

Cinch scowled. 'You'll be damn lucky

to find it,' he hollered. 'Getchur ass outta here.'

'Going. Going.' The Kid buttoned up his black slicker and sloshed through the mud to his gray pony. The horse stood spraddle-legged while he mounted. Its back seemed to lower by two inches as the Kid settled his butt in the saddle. He patted the horse's neck. 'Raining, old son, won't have much runnin' around to do tonight. Take 'er easy.' He neck-reined the pony toward the herd.

'Damn kid,' Cinch grumbled.

'He done a good thing, Cinch. Don't come down on him hard over it.' Monty added some hot coffee to his half-full cup.

'First thing ya know, he'll be a goldam squaw man.'

Monty threw a glance at Cinch. 'You got a problem with Injuns?'

'Goldam savages.'

'You better swallow that, Cinch. That bunch of Utes saved us time and probably money. And one of them's our blood brother. A man don't lie to his blood brother, even if he lies to his own ma. Lay off.'

Heck Lewis came splashing through the rain. The dim light of the lantern hanging under the tarp made his wet motley-brown horse look black. The heavens broke and water cascaded down upon Monty McCord, the drovers, 2,000 steers, and a brindle cow. No one wanted to move in the downpour, not the cattle, not the cowboys, and least of all the gaggle of gunmen led by Chico Valdez.

★ ★ ★

Chico'd hired seven gunmen in Ouray. He'd painted the job of stealing 2,000 head of cattle as an easy task — ride in with guns ready, strip the cowering drovers of their weapons, leave them bound with their own piggin strings, push the beeves to Uncompahgre Agency to turn them into easily carried cash. A hundred dollars each in easy cash. That's what Chico would have them think as they huddled beneath an overhang, trying to get out of the ferocious downpour.

Shorty Cluff pulled a bottle from his offside saddle-bag.

'Lay off the drink,' Chico said. 'Plenty of time for that after the cows are ours.'

'Shit,' Shorty said. But he put the bottle back.

'When do we hit the herd?' Hopalong Ford growled his question. On the ground, Ford walked with a pronounced limp. On a horse, he was more than a match for any rider.

'Before they cross the river,' Chico said. 'And I think we would be better to strike before the cows start down the wash. So, *amigos*, we strike the moment the rain begins to let up.'

A rumble of discontent passed through the gunmen. 'Better move pretty damn soon.'

'*Muy pronto*,' Chico said. He stared at each gunman in turn. 'Now is the time to look after your *pistolas*. Here, where the rain does not fall.' To add emphasis to his words, Chico pulled his own nickel-plated revolvers, one at a time, and checked their action and loads. Satisfied, he returned the Colts and withdrew a Winchester '73 from its saddle scabbard. The gun was one in a thousand and had cost him seventy-five dollars in Las Cruces. The lever worked smoother than silk, putting a cartridge into the breech. He added a shell from his cartridge belt to fill the magazine again. The rain eased off a bit. The gunmen made sure their weapons were ready to fire.

Shorty's hand strayed toward the bottle in his saddle-bag, but stopped when he saw that Chico watched. The Mexican gunman shook his head. Shorty sighed. He crossed his hands on the saddle horn, and pretended to sleep. Damn rain.

As the sky picked up a tinge of gray the rain throttled back to a misty drizzle. Chico pulled his hat down and reined his horse out from under the overhang. He'd not ridden twenty yards when he heard the roar of the Grand. The night of hard rain had filled the river and then some. Only a tenderfoot trail-boss would try driving cattle across that river, or so Chico Valdez reasoned. He smiled. Today he would be 2,000 head of cattle richer. Seagle assured him the agent at Uncompahgre was bought and paid for. He'd purchase any cattle Chico brought in, and brands were no problem. He turned his big black back toward the overhang.

'Time has come, *compadres*,' he said when he got close enough for them to hear.

'Yeah. That's what we've been waiting for.'

'None a them cowpokes better get'n my way. They do'n, they get shot quicker'n scat.'

'Shit, yeah. Time ta git them cows headed for Uncompahgre.'

Without thinking, the gunmen checked their weapons one more time, and gigged their mounts out into the misty drizzle.

★　★　★

In the gray of the dawn Monty stood by the fire, drinking his fifth cup of coffee, or was it the tenth? A bullet came out of nowhere and knocked his hat flying as it gouged a furrow along the side of his skull. He dropped like an ear-shot hog.

He came to in a sea of pain, his face in the mud of the night's rain. *The cows.* Monty couldn't help groaning when he tried to move his head. He held his breath, hoping that would reduce the pounding in his skull. It didn't, but he struggled to get his hands under his body so he could push on them and lift his torso from the mud. The maneuver took forever. After a while, he stopped trying. He brought an arm up to where he could use it as a pillow, and his consciousness slipped away.

The clouds moved on up the range,

leaving clear skies in their wake. By noon, the sun beat down as only it can in high Colorado country. Much of the mud from the night's rain had already dried, and there was nothing to indicate that 2,000 steers had occupied the land south of the Grand.

Again Monty McCord became aware of the pain in his head. Was it slightly less than before? Could he make it to his feet? He registered the smell of wet earth beneath him. There didn't seem to be any sounds. He raised his head, and immediately wished he hadn't. He gritted his teeth and placed his palms to the ground. This time he was able to push himself up into a kneeling position. He opened his eyes a crack.

Cinch McDougal lay face down in the remains of the fire. His precious coffee pot lay on its side. The hole in it matched the one in Cinch's back.

Shit.

Monty had the devil of a time turning his head. The smallest move-ment set off a tribe of demons armed with hammers to beat on the inside of his skull. He heard someone groaning and then realized it was his own voice. He ignored the pounding and slowly swiveled his head, squinting to reduce the pain caused by the noonday sun.

Cinch. Dead. Chuck wagon. Tipped over. Cows. Gone.

He spied a mound about a hundred yards off. Struggling to his feet, Monty took a careful step toward the lump of whatever it was. Another step. And another. The demons in his skull backed off a mite. He was able to open his eyes all the way. The mound turned into Gabriel Baca, sprawled, face to the sky, chest punctured with three bullet holes that he could see. Wrangler dead. Horses gone. Cows gone.

Shit. Boss needs money. Monty McCord made up his mind to follow the cows. His head cleared a bit, but all he could think about was getting the herd back. He returned to the chuck wagon. It lay on its side with a corner burnt. Someone had tossed a brand at it but the fire hadn't caught. Whoever raided the camp hadn't been thorough. Monty's gun was gone, but no one had sacked the chuck wagon.

'Sorry, old man,' Monty said to Cinch's body. 'I just ain't got what it takes to bury you and Gabe and whoever else is dead out there. I just gotta go get them cows.'

Monty squatted to pick up his hat, which must have cartwheeled away when the bullet knocked him down. He almost didn't make it back to his feet, but after gritting his teeth and holding his breath until the dizziness went away, he stood. The next job was to get all the way over to the chuck wagon, a good ten yards off, but it looked to Monty like ten hundred yards. 'Come on, cowboy,' he said aloud. 'Anywhere you're going, you get there a step at a time. Time to take that first step.'

He put a foot out about a foot, shifted his weight, then put the other foot out. 'Good,' he said. 'Now do it again.'

Before the sun was even halfway to the western horizon, Monty reached the chuck wagon. He found the raiders had been more thorough than he imagined. All the sowbelly was gone, and the sugar, too. Dried chilli peppers lay scattered around. A bag of flour was mostly poured out. It had maybe a cupful left. Better than nothing. Half a can of lard. Some hardtack. Dried beans, which Monty left where they lay. Not a gun or a bullet in sight. Cinch had said he had a .45–70 Winchester. Monty searched. No Winchester, but in a long box that looked like part of the wagon's floorboards, Monty found a .50 caliber Sharps buffalo gun. Heavy enough to use as a crutch if need be. Accurate to half a mile or more. He pulled the old rifle out and opened the action. It was loaded, so Monty popped the big cartridge out. It was clean. Cinch'd kept the old gun in shape. Bullets? Monty ran his hand along the inside of the hidy box. His fingers hit something soft. Cloth. He scrinched around until he could get a hold on the cloth thing and pull it out.

A small bag of bullets: .50–90 cartridges for the Sharps. Six in all. Monty McCord had seven shots, and a Barlow knife. He didn't have a canteen, and he didn't have a bedroll, but it wouldn't be the first time he'd lived off the land.

Canteen. Wait. Monty stood stock still. Cinch always had a canvas water bag hanging from the chuck wagon. Somehow the water in that bag was always cool. Left-hand side. Hung over a wooden hook. Problem. The chuck wagon lay left side down.

Monty moved carefully around the end of the wagon and peered down the top. No more than three feet forward of the end, a swatch of wet canvas stuck out from under the wagon. He made the three steps to the canvas. Was his head hurting less? He couldn't tell for sure, but he didn't seem to have as much trouble keeping his balance. He knelt by the patch of canvas. A good four inches stuck out, and the ground beneath it was wet and sticky. He grabbed hold of the canvas and pulled. At first it hung up, but when Monty pulled harder, it moved.

He took a new hold, this time with both hands. Then he let go. He sat down with the canvas between his legs. He put his boots against the wagon top. Again he grabbed the canvas with both hands, leaned back until his arms were straight, then pushed with his legs. Hard. An inch. Two. Slowly, slowly, shifting grip several times, Monty pulled the water bag out from under the wagon.

Finally the bag was free, except for its rope handle. Monty wasted no more strength pulling on the rope. He fished the Barlow knife from his pocket and cut the rope. Now he had a canteen. The sun neared the treetops west of the camp.

Monty cut the flour sack like he'd so often cut gunnysacks to make nosebags for the horses. There seemed to be about a pound of flour in the bottom. He'd not eaten since early morning, but the ache in his head stole any appetite. *Nothing to do now but go.*

With good drovers, a herd could make fifteen miles a day. A man walks about three miles in an hour, steady. A long day would give him about thirty miles. Monty rigged a new rope handle on the water bag with a piggin string. The bag had a little water in it, too. He slung the water bag over his right shoulder so it rested on his left hip. The flour sack hung on the other side. He habitually carried matches. He had a full sack of Bull Durham. He had a tally book and a stub of a pencil. He had flour and a little water. He had a Sharps .50 rifle with seven bullets. He took a deep breath. He adjusted his greasy old Stetson to a more comfortable position.

With the Sharps across his shoulders, the flour hanging on one side and the water bag on the other, Monty McCord started out after his boss's cows.

11

Monty found Heck Lewis face down in the trampled mud left by the herd. He had a bullet hole almost dead center of his back. The day was nearly gone. The gold and brilliant oranges of the Colorado mountain sunset had faded and the evening star shone bright in the western sky. The air was clean. No smoke. No dust. No smells that didn't belong.

'Sorry, feller,' Monty said to Heck's body. He lifted his head. 'Sorry, fellers,' he hollered. He just couldn't take the time to search all over the place they'd held the herd. He had to get on. If he was the only one left, so be it. If not, well, all the men rode for the brand, and that meant sooner or later they'd show up wherever the cattle were. Shifting the Sharps to a more comfortable position across his shoulders,

Monty McCord set out after the herd once more.

The moon rose, big and smoky-gold-colored as it cleared the pines to the east. As it got higher, it turned white, and the light it shed turned everything blue. Monty had no problem keeping to the trail of 2,000 cows. He didn't try to read sign, he didn't try to second-guess the owlhoots, and he didn't try any fancy gaits. He just slogged along, putting one foot in front of the other, until he tripped over a little rock and fell.

So good to lie down. So good. Just a minute of rest. Monty put his head down on his arms and rested. Just a minute.

He opened his eyes to find the moon high in the sky. How long had he slept? Three hours? Four?

His throat was dry and his head felt like a horse had stepped on it, but the demons with their hammers were gone. He sat up and took a sip from the water bag. Stale. Wet. Wonderful. He used the

Sharps as a prop to help him get to his feet. 'Come on, old son,' he said aloud. 'Gotta get them cows.'

Again he put one foot in front of the other and followed the broad trail of 2,000 cows. He didn't find any more dead cowboys, but he didn't find any live ones either. And the Sharps was starting to wear holes in his muscles where it rested across his shoulders.

Off to the east, he heard the call of a timber wolf. Another answered from a place south of the first. A pack gathering? *Wolves don't hunt men. Do they?*

He paid no more attention to the howls, except to note that they seemed to be moving north toward the river. A step. Another step. A third. Spending life on a horse like a cowboy should hadn't prepared Monty for this long-distance march. His boots, with their underslung heels, weren't designed for footwork either. He limped as the sun rose, and when it cleared the western tree line, he found a chair-high rock to sit on. He put the toe of his right boot behind the heel of his left one and prised it off. The cool air felt good, but he didn't like the blood spots on his sock. He used the toes of his left foot to remove his right boot. He found that heaven meant having his hot, tired feet free of constricting boot leather. *Right now, I'd give a whole gold eagle to have a good pair of Ute moccasins.*

Wiggling his toes and heaving sighs of bliss, Monty used his rest time to inspect his surroundings. The trampled trail of the herd moved almost exactly back the way it had come, which made sense because with Deerstone's help, Monty had chosen the easiest way north for those cows.

As the morning sun warmed Monty, a meadowlark hovered above the grass a few yards away, whistling and warbling its mountain song. *A man would never know there was owlhoots ahead who left H Bar H and Flying W cowboys lying dead in their own blood.*

Monty dreaded pulling his boots

back on, but he'd spent more than enough time on the rock. Fingers through the loops on the boots' stovepipe shafts, he shoved his sore feet back into their torture chambers one at a time. It might hurt to walk in the boots, but it'd hurt a lot more walking barefoot. *Where are the goldam Utes when you need them?*

Two hours Monty limped onward on the tracks of the cows. The Sharps weighed slightly less than half a ton. The cup of flour weighed at least ten pounds. The near-empty water bag weighed more than it possibly could have plumb full. Monty had to consciously keep himself from dropping the heavy things by the side of the herd's trail.

He stopped about noon in the shade of a tall ponderosa, and built a hatful of fire with some of the tree's needles and a couple of larger branches broken from a deadfall. He cut a long shoot from a juniper and trimmed it with his Barlow knife. Time to eat. He mixed flour with a little water in his tin cup to make dough, which he rolled between his palms and wrapped around the juniper stick in a spiral. Took a good quarter of an hour to cook the dough, but when it was golden brown all over, Monty broke it off the stick and wolfed it down. Absolutely the best bread he'd had in thirty-two years of living.

Reluctantly, Monty stamped out the little fire and made sure there was not so much as a single spark left. Sharps across his shoulders, he trudged on. The pain in his head receded to a dull ache, but the pain in his feet took on bonfire proportions. He had to get the Flying W and H Bar H stock back. No two ways about it.

He couldn't tell if he was gaining on the herd. He couldn't hear anything that sounded like cows ahead. He heard the *shack-sheck-sheck* of jays in the pines. He caught the glimpses of cottontail rabbits diving into the underbrush. A hawk coasted high above.

Monty had to think himself along. *Right foot forward. Left foot forward.* He focused on the cows to take his mind from the burning pain of his blistered feet.

Monty ate another twist of plain-roasted bread just before sundown. Maybe he was gaining on the herd. The cowpies left by the steers looked fresher, but he still heard nothing that sounded like cows. He carried the heavy old Sharps in his right hand now. The big gun had rubbed his shoulders raw. The blisters on his feet had long since given up their outer skin, leaving raw patches the size of Mexican silver dollars on his heels.

He had to force himself to rise, stamp out the little fire, take up the now flat water bag and nearly depleted flour sack, retrieve the Sharps from where it leaned against a pine tree, and once more strike out to follow the herd. But follow it he did. Monty McCord had no intention of allowing a bunch of bushwhackers to make off with the critters Ellen Wilson had put in his charge. None.

He plodded on through the night, stumbling over a stone here and a bush there. Sometimes he stumbled over his own feet. Sometimes he wandered into stands of jackpines when he didn't watch where he was headed. Sometimes he woke to find himself standing in the middle of the tracks made by 2,000 cows, legs spread apart and Sharps butt to the ground, forming a tripod of support.

Doggedly he continued, not stopping to rest and, after the flour gave out, not stopping for food. He tossed the flour sack away, getting rid of even its slight extra weight.

More and more he felt like he was walking in a tunnel with darkness closing in on both sides. He didn't think of the futility in what he did, he thought only of the boss and how she depended on him to get the cash money she needed to save the Flying W and the H Bar H spreads.

Just before dawn he tripped over a rock and fell face down. He didn't even try to get up. His breath came in ragged gasps and for the first time he could remember, he cried. Not the yowl of a youngster, but great heaving sobs with hardly any sound. Despair of ever catching up with the stolen herd filled his soul. Despair at his inability to do the job the boss had asked him to do. Despair at the dead cow-pokes who lay under the brassy Colorado sky and waited for buzzards and coyotes to pick their bones clean. Despair. Despair. Despair.

He might be better off dead. Maybe. But there was no one else to give the rustlers hell. No one to make sure they didn't get away with the boss's cows.

A plan. That's what he needed. A plan. He lay where he'd fallen, more asleep than awake. More unconscious than conscious. More gone than present. His mind wandered and he couldn't seem to focus on a plan.

'You gotta be the laziest cahoot that

ever ramrodded a trail herd.'

Monty heard the voice in the distance. It sounded familiar. Very familiar. Who? He scrinched up his eyes and tried to think. What was that smell? Coffee? Here? He struggled to make sense of it all.

'Hey, Monty. Don't be such a lazy ass.'

Monty lifted his ten-ton head from the ground. '*Unngh harruuumph*,' he said.

'Monty!'

A shout. Someone jostled his shoulders. He tried to bat the hands away but couldn't seem to control his own arms.

'*Grumph eergle*,' he said.

'Monty. Hear me? Wake up, cowboy. Look alive!'

Monty shook his head. He cracked his eyelids and winced at the brilliant sunlight. 'Cows?' he said.

'Drove off. Here. Coffee.'

Monty took a deep breath. 'I know the cows's drove off,' he said, steel creeping back into his voice. At last he could open his eyes full wide and find out who was hollering at him. He clambered to his feet, never letting go of the old Sharps. The old rifle held under his right arm, with his left hand on the hammer, ready to ear it back to full cock, Monty turned to face his tormenter.

'Kid?'

'Yep. Me'n Badger Son.' The Kid held out a cup of coffee. 'We brung Baron along. Them owlhoots shot the remuda horse you was on, but we gotchur saddle'n stuff off it. Owlhoots took the Winchester. Sorry.'

Monty sipped at the coffee. Strong. Black. His head got clearer. 'S'OK, Kid. I got me a long-shooting Sharps. I seen Cinch and Gabe dead. Heck, too. Any more?'

'Me'n the boy was on the far side of the herd when they came,' the Kid said. 'We faded back into the trees, and they never looked for us. Deerstone's up ahead. Billy Bob's at the Ute camp along with Aaron and Josie. They got bullet holes in 'em.'

'Four of us, then?'

'Four?'

'Yeah. You and me. Deerstone and the Radley boy.'

'I reckon not. We got Badger Boy and Paatangwaci. We got the whole Ute band if we want 'em.'

Monty tossed the dregs from the coffee cup and gave it back to the Kid. He strode over to Baron, patted him once on the nose, and climbed aboard. He hung his water bag over the saddle horn and shoved the old Sharps into the boot. 'Just think for a minute about what you said, Kid.'

The Kid scrunched up his shoulders and puffed up like a banty rooster. 'What'd I say?'

'You said the Utes would fight with us.'

'They would. Badger Son's my blood brother.'

'What do you think'd happen if a bunch of Utes shot up a bunch of white men? You think them in town would stand for that? We'd have another Meeker's War on our hands afore you could count all the way to ten.' Monty neck-reined Baron on to the herd's trail. 'See what I'm saying, Kid?'

The Kid rode up on one side of Monty, Badger Son on the other. 'OK. I can see whatchur saying. But they don't have to do no killing. I mean, you would still be walking if Badger Son hadn't stole old Baron right out from under them bandits' noses. Way I see it, the Utes don't never have to show even one feather.'

Monty cracked a little smile. 'Keep 'em out of sight, Kid. Plumb outta sight.' He held out a hand. 'Damn coffee turns a man dry. Got a swallow of water for a thirsty trail boss?'

Badger Son handed him a water skin. 'You drink,' he said.

'Good white man words,' Monty said. He took a swallow and a half, and gave the skin back. 'My thanks, brother of the Kid. Ride with care. Do not let the white men see you.'

Badger Son snorted.

'Here.' The Kid held out a strip of jerky.

Monty took it with a nod of thanks. He reined Baron onto the trail left by Ellen Watson's cows, wrestled to bite off a chunk of jerky, and settled down to chew as he rode after the herd. The Kid followed. Badger Son disappeared.

'Badger Son's got an idea,' the Kid said.

Monty rode on, head down, jaws working at the jerky.

'Wanna hear it?'

'Hear what?' Monty spoke around the plug of dried meat in his mouth. He couldn't seem to get enough saliva to moisten it up right.

'Badger Son's idea.'

'How in hell did he ever come up with an idea?'

'My brother's got lots of ideas,' the Kid said. 'Wish I had as many. But I'm better with a six-gun than he is, so I reckon maybe we're kind of even.'

'So what's his idea?'

'Badger Son figures we oughta steal the horses.'

'No guff.'

'Yeah. Steal the remuda. Them owl-hoots's got big plugs that ain't much good as cowponies. Without the remuda, they won't last a week.'

'We ain't got a week.' Monty bit off another small piece of jerky. Baron walked straight ahead, holding to the cow trail.

'Then we get 'em quicker.'

'I'll tell you what. I'm riding up on that herd to take a chunk outta them what bushwhacked us and took the boss's cows. Your brother can steal the remuda if he gets the chance, but I'm riding in. As soon as I'm in Sharps range, I'm gonna start shooting.'

'Reckon I'll go along then,' the Kid said. 'If it's OK with you, boss.'

'You done good to get Baron back for me, Kid. Proud to have you ride alongside me.'

'Cain't catch no cows jawing. Let's

move.' The Kid gigged his pony into a ground-eating lope.

Baron followed the pony, then passed him. Baron never liked for another horse to get ahead of him.

Monty and the Kid kept their horses in a lope-trot rhythm as the sun traveled across a cloudless sky. Grasshoppers flew out from under the horses' hoofs, and once in a while a bee would zoom by, intent on gathering nectar from sumac and butterfly weed, mountain dandelions and wild clover. The riders paid the insects no mind. They were after something a lot bigger than the odd yellowjacket, something that carried a sting of death in holstered six-guns and lever-action Winchesters.

They rode on.

12

They heard the cows just before sundown.

Monty pulled up and the Kid reined in beside him.

'You go tell your brother to do his damndest with the remuda,' Monty said. 'I'll watch tonight, and hit 'em just before sunrise.'

'He knows what to do without me having to tell him. I'll just stick around.'

Monty glared at the Kid, who returned his look with a deadpan stare, as if daring Monty to tell him to ride off. ''Zat so? May be some shooting. Them owlhoots killed a bunch of my cowpokes. They gotta pay.'

'I got a gun 'n' I know how to use it.'

'No fast-draw contest, Kid. But anyway, come along if you wanna.'

No reason to ride at a lope now. Monty took Baron west of the herd.

The rustlers would naturally watch their back trail, even if they thought they'd killed all the drovers. And they were missing horses, so they'd be on the lookout for Indians. He rode west for a good mile, then reined Baron in. The sounds of the herd no longer reached him. The Kid stopped alongside.

Monty spoke in a low voice, scarcely more than a whisper. 'We'll ride south from here,' he said. 'Them owlhoots might push them critters all night, but I'm figuring they'll bed down the cows for a while.'

'If we get ahead of them, we can find a good place to hunker down,' the Kid said. 'Pick 'em off. Easy.'

'Killing men ain't never easy,' Monty said. 'But these's killed Flying W and H Bar H riders. We owe them.'

'I'll say.' The Kid gigged his horse south at a trot.

Monty followed, Baron striding forward with his long single-foot, which was nearly as fast as most horses' trot.

Some time after midnight, the riders turned east.

Monty juggled with just where the herd was headed. *They can't drive them critters onto our range. Denver?* Denver could swallow a herd of 2,000 without blinking an eye. But getting a big herd through Monarch Pass would be a tough job for seasoned drovers, never mind a bunch of gunnies. In the direction they were going, the only other place that bought big bunches of cows was Uncompahgre Indian Agency.

When they stopped to let the horses rest and grab a few mouthfuls of rich mountain grass, Monty voiced his thoughts.

'Where're these rustlers expecting to sell a couple thousand steers? Denver, maybe, but I'm thinking Uncompahgre. General Adams is there, 'cause they're getting ready to move Utes all the way to Utah. He'll need cows to supply the army and the Indians. That's what I figure. He's probably got word that Flying W and H Bar H cows are coming, so he won't do more than look at the brands. The rustlers could spin any old story about why Croft or Blake ain't with the herd. No one in Uncompahgre knows us anyhow.' He chewed on his upper lip as he thought about it. The Indian Agency was logical. Plumb logical.

'So what?' the Kid said.

'Dunno.'

'Go straight to Uncompahgre?'

'Thought about that,' Monty said, pulling at his moustache with thumb and forefinger. 'Don't want them cowboy killers to get away without a taste of what they give out.'

Monty pulled a stalk of foxtail and chewed on it. 'If they head straight for the agency, they'll have to cross Flying W range. Blake'll have line riders out. So'll Croft. Anyone with any smarts'll know that. So once they get the critters across Green River, they'll bend around to the east and go up the plateau to the agency. That's how I figure it, anyway.'

The Kid stared at the ground like he

was watching his cayuse eat grass. He took a deep breath. 'Boss, you're as good as they come, gun or fist. Whatever you decide, I'll be right there.'

'Let us git across the Green and up on that little rocky knoll due south of the ford. From there, we can see what they do.'

'Lead on.'

Monty led, and he and the Kid crossed the Green, which ran shin deep on a tall horse, even after the rain, then they loped toward the knoll and its cover of tumbled boulders and piñon pines.

They tied their horses to low limbs of scrub oak and made their way up the back of the knoll. Bellied down in the scramble of boulders, Monty squinted toward the Green. 'How far you figure the ford, Kid? Your eyes're better'n mine.'

'Half a mile. No more'n three-quarters.'

'Gitchur head down.'

They watched from between the boulders, taking care not to skyline anything unnatural, like a hat or a head or a gun barrel.

The sun'd been up for a good two hours before any sign of the herd showed. As Monty expected, the brindle cow led. She stopped at the edge of the ford to take a long drink, and the steers crowded in behind. Riders to the left and right of the herd shouted and slapped the ends of their reins at the rumps of the steers.

'Hey, Monty,' the Kid rasped.

Monty looked at the Kid, his eyebrow arched in a question.

'See that feller with the black hat? The one with two guns?'

Monty nodded.

'That's Chico Valdez.'

'You know him?'

This time the Kid nodded. 'Seen 'im down to Texas once. I was only ten years old, but I seen him. He killed a man that day. Laughed a lot. Like it was a fun thing to do.'

'Who'd he kill? Anyone you knew?'

'My ma's only brother. Uncle Fred thought he was something with a gun. Never got it clear of the holster. Valdez shot him right in the middle of the forehead. Almost offhand about it.' The kid lay silent behind his boulder for some time. Then he said, 'I'd like to get even with that gun-sharp for what he done.'

Monty nodded. 'You keep your eye on him.'

The steers crowded up behind the brindle cow and she crossed the river to put space between them and her. The steers followed like calves following their mamas.

Monty settled down over the sights of the old Sharps. He'd never shot the old rifle, so he didn't know its peculiarities. But he trusted the loving care Cinch had given the old gun. No one would keep a rifle in such pristine condition unless it hit what it was pointed at.

The kid checked his pistols.

Suddenly Monty stood up and fired a

shot into the air. 'Valdez,' he roared. 'Chico Valdez!'

At half a mile, Valdez most likely couldn't hear Monty's shout, but he could see. And the blue smoke from the old Sharps hung in the clear Colorado air.

The man in black pulled away from the herd and rode his blaze-faced black horse toward the knoll. Monty reloaded the Sharps. Now he had only six rounds. Valdez kept his hands crossed on the saddle horn, but the butt of his left-hand Colt was only inches away from his gloved right hand. The herd kept coming.

Fifty yards away, Valdez reined the black to a stop.

'I'll not bushwhack a man,' Monty said. 'Even if he's driving my cows.' He paused a moment.

Valdez sat his horse without comment.

'Your fine horse looks about played out, Valdez. Makes me think maybe you got no way to give him a rest.'

'What is your business, line rider? We have cattle to deliver and must be on our way.'

'Them's my cows.'

'*Perdon, señor*. These creatures go to Uncompahgre Agency, where Señor Barry Seagle waits with gold coins to pay the riders . . . and me. I think you cannot take these creatures by yourself. And I think an honorable man such as you, *señor*, would not shoot a man in the back.' Valdez reined his horse around and rode slowly back toward the herd.

'Monty,' the Kid whispered from his hiding place. 'You just gonna let him ride away?'

Monty grinned, but the expression on his face was not pleasant to see. 'Got me an idea, Kid. Got me an idea.'

★   ★   ★

Barry Seagle sat in the chair in front of Indian Agent Carl Riess's desk like he sat at a card table. Relaxed, yet alert, a half-smile on his lips, bonhomie in his eyes, and lust in his heart. Lust for dollars. Twenty dollars a head for 2,000 steers.

'No sign of your cows, Barry.'

Seagle's half-smile widened into a full one. 'Soon, Carl. Soon.'

'You know I'll have to pay with a government bank draft, don't you?'

'Wells Fargo will turn it into cash for a fee. No problem.' Seagle snapped his fingers as if just coming up with an idea. 'In fact, Carl, as I need to get back to Watsonville, why don't you give me the draft now? I could get it turned into hard cash while we're waiting for the herd. Make it for forty thousand, twenty dollars a head. I'll refund you a dollar a head as soon as I get the cash.'

'Would you be trying to bribe a government official?'

'Not at all. A dollar a head's not bribery, it's a gratuity, a well earned gratuity.'

Riess kept a straight face, but his eyes

showed his approval of Seagle's proposal. 'Highly unusual,' he said. 'We usually pay after the stock has been corralled and properly counted.'

'Well, just to be sure, if there are less than two thousand, I'll return the full price of the missing steers. If there are more than two thousand, I'll say 'Paid in full'.'

Still with a straight face, Riess said, 'That seems to be in the government's favor.' He opened a desk drawer and withdrew a pad of blank bank drafts. He trimmed the quill of a turkey feather, dipped it in the inkwell let into the top of his desk, and pulled the pad of drafts close. 'To Bartholomew Seagle,' he said as he wrote. 'The sum of forty thousand dollars only, for two thousand head of beef cattle delivered to Uncompahgre Agency, State of Colorado.' He wrote in the date, sanded the draft, and handed it to Barry Seagle. In a voice completely devoid of inflection, Reiss said, 'If the steers don't show up,

Barry, I wouldn't be surprised if someone found you outside the Bucket of Blood with a Ute arrow in your gizzard.' He extracted another form from the papers that lay on his desk. 'Just to be sure things are as they seem, put your signature on this receipt.' He dipped the pen and wrote, again speaking aloud the words. 'Received: Forty thousand dollars, payment in full for two thousand two- and three-year-old steers wearing Flying W and H Bar H brands.' He sanded the receipt and turned it around so Seagle could sign it.

Seagle forced a chuckle. 'No need to get histrionic, Carl. The cattle will be here.' He dipped the pen in the inkwell and signed the receipt with a flourish, then held the bank draft up. 'If you'll excuse me, I'll stroll over to the fort and get Wells Fargo to turn this into cash.'

'Just make sure you get enough to deliver the gratuity you spoke of.'

'Absolutely. Absolutely.'

'And don't forget about the Ute arrow.'

'I'll be leaving, then,' Seagle said. He stood and offered his hand.

Reiss rose, and stepped back from his desk. He ignored Seagle's outstretched hand. 'I look forward to your speedy return,' he said. 'Good day.'

★   ★   ★

'Kid,' Monty said. 'I'm gonna ask you to make a fast, hard ride. Now here's what I'm gonna do. Valdez said he's taking the beeves to Uncompahgre Agency. I'm gonna believe him, and I'm gonna get there first. But one of me ain't gonna be enough. I want you to ride for the Army post outside the agency and get a telegram to Marshal Slade. Tell him everything you know, and get him to come to Uncompahgre Agency. Meet me there. Got that?'

The Kid nodded. He stuck out a hand and Monty shook it. 'You can trust me,' the Kid said. 'I'll get the job done.'

'I do, Kid. I do. Now git. And stay outta sight of that herd.'

The Kid squirmed down the back of the knoll as Flying W and H Bar H steers plowed across the Green, following the brindle cow. Monty watched until he could count the number of riders with the herd. Eight. Chico Valdez and seven more.

There was no remuda and no chuck wagon. Monty grinned. The owlhoots would be mighty lucky to get all the steers to Uncompahgre. The steers had crossed the river following the brindle cow, but things would get tougher as they pushed up and over the plateau.

Monty waited until the herd passed, then made his way to the river to refill his water bag. Baron held up well and was used to long rides. He grazed while Monty got water, and was more than ready to go when his rider mounted.

Not quite a hundred miles to Uncompahgre if a man could fly

straight like a crow. Monty lifted Baron into the swift single-foot the horse could keep up for hours. At night, he stopped to let Baron rest and to find some food — clover, dandelion greens, wild lettuce, heated in his coffee cup. He even found a few wild raspberries. If a man knew the country, he had no need to carry biscuits and bacon. He was even able to sleep a little. But dawn found him on his way, Baron moving well at a tireless single-foot pace.

Every army post had its hogtown. Fort Hays was not different. Monty rode Baron down the single dusty street of the Hays hogtown late on the second day after leaving Chico Valdez and the Flying W herd at Green River. Baron easily covered forty to fifty miles a day, depending on the terrain, but the herd would do well to make fifteen. A single row of poles marched away toward Monarch Pass bearing the fragile wire of the army's telegraph network. With luck, the Kid would have already gotten word to Marshal Slade.

The only decent-looking saloon in hogtown was the Silver Dollar. Its plank-and-batten walls still showed the yellow of fresh-cut pine. In a year, they'd be slate-gray. Monty rode past the saloon, looking for anything reminiscent of a livery barn. It turned out to be a little shed with four stalls and a corral made of aspen poles. Baron got the last stall, a bait of oat-stalk hay, and a quart of oats that cost almost as much as a fifth of rye whiskey.

Monty walked back to the Silver Dollar, the old Sharps a solid weight in the crook of his left arm. Each step raised miniature dust devils and he missed the familiar weight of a Peacemaker on his hip. A man could never tell what might happen, especially in hogtown.

13

The Silver Dollar had no such trappings as batwing doors. No windows facing the street, either. Monty turned the knob on the ordinary front door and stepped into familiar surroundings. A long bar down the right-hand side of the room, a row of tables down the left. Card players occupied the two tables farthest from the door. Half a dozen men stood hipshot at the bar, glasses in front to them, some full, some nearly empty. After a moment's hesitation, Monty shifted the Sharps to his right hand and made his way to the bar.

Men looked up when Monty passed, their eyes stopping at the peculiar slant of his hat. After he got a drink, he'd wander over to the stockade and get the sawbones to take a look at the crease in his hair. He took a place at the end of the bar closest to the door.

The bartender sauntered up the bar to stand before Monty. He raised an eyebrow.

'Something in a bottle,' Monty said, 'unopened.'

'We got whiskey,' the bartender said. 'No bottles.'

'What's in it?'

'Ain't nobody died here of whiskey poisoning.'

'Then I'll have a shot.'

The barkeep sauntered back down the bar to a keg set up on a stand about waist high. He slid the top over and used a dipper to pour three fingers of cloudy amberish liquid into a whiskey glass. He set the glass on the bar and gave it a shove. It zoomed past three dedicated drinkers and came to a stop in front of Monty.

'Four bits,' the 'keep said.

Monty picked up the glass and brought it to his nose. Raw spirits. Plug tobacco. Tabasco sauce. Real frontier whiskey, and here it was 1880. He ventured a sip. It burned from lips to stomach and beyond. He felt the fiery liquid as it rolled through his innards. Then the fire became a warmth and he took a second sip.

The barkeep stood in front of him, arms akimbo. He stuck his hand out, palm up. 'Four bits.'

Monty dug into his pocket and came up with a few coins. He plonked them on the bar and separated out a quarter, two dimes, and a nickel, and pushed them toward the barkeep.

'You make fair-to-middling whiskey,' Monty said. 'What's the secret?'

'Wouldn't you like to know? Drink up.'

'What's this burg called, anyway?'

'Fort Uncompahgre's hogtown's all I've ever heard.'

'Where can I find a room? Didn't see no hotel.'

'Ain't got one. Betty Alice's is the tarpaper place back down the road about half a mile. Rooms with or without. She'll let you sleep on the front room floor, too, cheap.'

Monty killed half the glass of whiskey in a gulp. Didn't burn as much, felt a hell of a lot better. His headache receded to the level of a distant memory. The bartender leaned against the wall. The dedicated drinkers studied the liquor in their glasses. *Quiet place for a saloon*. Monty took another gulp of firewater. 'Things always this quiet?' he asked the barkeep.

'Sojers get off duty, they raise a little ruckus,' the 'keep said.

The door swung open. Monty threw a glance over his left shoulder to see who it was. Barry Seagle strode into the saloon with a face that looked ready to cloud up and rain.

Monty turned away, hoping Seagle would not recognize him.

The gambler made straight for the middle of the bar. 'Shit, Clevis,' he said. 'How come things never go my way? Whiskey, goldammit. A full glass, if you don't mind.'

The barkeep said nothing, but

walked to the keg and ladled a whiskey glass brimming full. He brought it carefully back and set it in front of Seagle. Two dedicated drinkers stood between Seagle and Monty McCord. 'Dollar,' the barkeep said.

'Shit. Goldam home-made horse piss,' Seagle said.

The barkeep reached for the glass of whiskey. 'No one's forcing you, Seagle,' he said.

Seagle grabbed the glass. 'OK. OK. Shit. The whole goldam country's after my goldam money.'

'You drink my whiskey. I take your money. Fair trade,' the barkeep said.

Seagle pulled a poke from an inner pocket of his coat. To Monty, it looked like it had more than a dollar in it. Seagle extracted a coin, a double eagle. He plonked it on the bar.

'You're looking flush, Seagle,' the bartender said. He smiled, but didn't take his eyes from the poke.

'Sold a herd,' Seagle said.

Monty's ears pricked up. The herd

wasn't even in sight, and Seagle had it sold?

'Then whacha bitching about?' The barkeep grinned, but his eyes had a hard sparkle. 'Ain't seen no herd, Seagle. How'd you work it? Selling ghosts now?'

'The cows'll be along directly, never you worry.' Seagle held out the double eagle. 'A dollar outta this,' he said.

The barkeep took the coin and went to his change box. He rattled the money in it around for a while, then came back with an eagle and seven silver dollars. 'This's all I've got right now,' he said. 'You can drink up the difference, or wait a while. I'll have more later.'

Grumbling under his breath, Seagle pocketed the dollars and put the gold eagle in the poke. He carefully raised the glass and took two healthy swallows. 'Damn. Damn. Damn. And double damn.'

'You're awful sour for a man with that much money in his pocket.'

Seagle took two more swallows of

whiskey. 'Ought to be a lot more. A helluva lot more.'

The barkeep said nothing more, and Seagle just drank. Monty kept his shoulders hunched and his nose in his drink. A few minutes later, Seagle began to pay attention to the card games at the far end of the room. Then he ordered a refill and sauntered over to watch.

Monty took the opportunity to leave the Silver Dollar. As he rode toward Fort Uncompahgre and the Indian Agency, he mulled over what he knew. The Flying W and H Bar H herd seemed to have been sold by Barry Seagle, without even one beef setting foot on Uncompahgre land. But Seagle wasn't happy about the money. He had a poke full, but not a big enough poke to hold $40,000 in double eagles. Monty wondered how much Seagle had promised Chico Valdez.

As Monty mounted the steps to the porch in front of the Uncompahgre Agency sutler's store, the tame Ute who squatted to one side of the door said, 'Boss. Cows come soon. Maybe sunrise.'

Monty did a double take. 'That you, Badger Son?'

'I watch, boss. You take easy.'

'Where's the Kid?'

Badger Son shrugged. 'Never worry,' he said. 'My brother will do what he must.'

This time Monty shrugged. 'So be it.' He stalked into the sutler's store.

The woman behind the counter looked up as Monty entered. 'Good afternoon, sir,' she said, her voice a mellow contralto.

Monty stopped dead. His mouth went dry and he couldn't say a word. He'd never seen a woman so . . . Even in his mind he couldn't find words to describe her. It wasn't that she was some kind of blazing beauty: she wasn't. But there was something about her. An aura. A quiet confidence. A pleasant expression that wasn't just the look of good will a shopkeeper offers a customer. She looked content, satisfied, at peace, from the inside out. There wasn't a worry line anywhere on her face. Her clothing was simple and modest. No lace. No jewelry. No embroidery. Her hand, with its long, graceful fingers, brushed a stray strand of dark-brown hair away from her face and put it in place behind her ear.

'How may I help you, sir?' she said. Again, her contralto voice shivered Monty to the toes of his worn boots.

'Uuum,' he said.

She looked at him directly, her eyes wide in anticipation. *Surely there is something I can do for you*, the clear hazel pupils seemed to say.

'Um. Um. Miss. Er. I was wondering,' Monty said, his ears turning red beneath his dirty canted Stetson.

'Yes, sir?' Her eyes looked straight into his. She didn't seem to notice his dirty clothing, the old Sharps buffalo gun, his unwashed odor, or the steep tilt of his hat. She seemed to see only him, a simple honest cowman.

'Uum. I was wondering if there was a sawbones at this here camp. At Fort Uncompahgre, I mean.'

'A doctor, sir? A physician? A surgeon? Are you wounded, sir?'

'I got shot,' Monty said. 'Sometimes my head still aches.'

'I heard that Dr Forbush, the surgeon at Fort Uncompahgre, was called to Denver, sir.'

Monty's face fell. He knew he should get the crease in his skull looked at, but if the sawbones was gone . . .

'May I look at your wound, sir?'

'Not much to it,' Monty said. 'Ain't had no one look at it for three days or so, and I ain't dead yet.'

'Still.' Her brow knitted in a frown of concern. 'Perhaps I could at least dress it properly.' She hesitated. 'And wash the dried blood from your neck. We have shirts here, if you wish to purchase one to take the place of the bloody and dusty one you have on.' Her smile and soft contralto voice removed any sting from her words.

'Well. Hell. I mean . . . Pardon me, miss. Usually all I got to talk to is cows. I completely forget manners. If I ever knew any, that is.'

'I'm not 'miss',' she said. 'Please call me Ann. That's my name. Really. Nothing complicated like Antoinette or Annabelle. Just plain, no frills, Ann.' She smiled again.

'Uum. Well. Er. Ann.' He took off his Stetson and indicated the crease in his scalp with an index finger. 'Bushwhacked. I reckon the shooter figures I'm dead.'

Ann stood on tiptoes to look at the furrow along the side of Monty's head. 'It would be much easier, sir, if you were to sit down on the stool by the counter,' she said.

Monty began to realize what a mess he was. His face hadn't seen a razor for what, a week? More? On a drive, a man didn't shave much, and he didn't change clothes until the end of the trail. Just wasn't done.

'I'm going to heat some water,' Ann

said. 'It won't take but a minute.' She disappeared into the back of the sutler's store, leaving Monty McCord sitting on a stool with his hat in his hand and the old Sharps buffalo gun leaning against the counter.

True to her word, Ann came back only a few moments after she'd left. She carried a pan of steaming water in one hand and a cup of steaming coffee in the other. 'I thought perhaps you'd like some coffee,' she said. 'I didn't think to ask, so I just brought some.' She set the cup on the counter with its handle toward Monty.

He wondered what she thought of the whiskey on his breath. Was that why she brought the coffee? Was she afraid? 'Uum,' he said, 'maybe I'd better . . . '

'Sir!' She put her hands on her hips, her arms akimbo. 'You just sit still for a few moments. I'm not a harridan and I won't take a bite out of you. Now. Have a sip of the coffee while I get ready to look after that gunshot wound.'

'Yes'm.'

She stamped her foot. 'Sir! Did I not tell you my name is Ann? I most certainly am not some ma'am whom you do not know. Am I?'

'No, 'm, I mean, Ann.'

'Good.' She folded a piece of flour sack into a pad, which she wet in the pan of water. 'Hold still now.' Gently she began removing dirt, pine needles, flotsam and jetsam that dried blood held captured in Monty's head of thick, dark-brown hair.

Monty couldn't remember ever having felt a woman's tender touch. Not the kind of careful ministrations Ann gave him, anyhow. He sat very still, even though the coffee was getting cold.

'Time to have some coffee,' Ann said. 'It should be cool enough.'

'Yes'm, er, Ann. Thank you.' Monty covered his unease by taking the coffee cup in both hands and gulping at the black brew.

Ann giggled. 'You must be very thirsty, sir. Have you traveled far since that dastardly person shot you?'

'Um. Well. Yeah, a ways, I reckon.' Monty never was a fast talker, but being so close to Ann, not a dove in any sense of the word, being able to breath in the warm fragrance of her and being able to listen to the comforting contralto of her voice had him nearly tongue-tied. He covered his discomfiture by lifting the coffee cup and sipping at its contents.

Ann wet the cloth again and returned to cleaning Monty's wound. 'Would you mind terribly if I were to clip the hair away from the vicinity of your wound, sir? That would allow me to see it better.'

'Unh-uh.'

'Do you mean it's all right?'

'Uh-huh.'

'You certainly do not talk very much, sir. I can hardly understand what you mean.'

'Sorry. You can cut my hair any way you please,' Monty said.

Ann snipped Monty's hair, exposing the furrow the bullet had plowed in his scalp. She clucked at the sight, but tenderly removed all dirt and foreign matter with the cloth, which she repeatedly wetted in the pan of hot water.

At last she stepped back. 'That's all I can do, sir. There's a hard scab covering the place where the bullet scraped along your head. I shouldn't try to remove it.'

She gasped, as if hit by a sudden idea. 'Just a moment, sir.' She bustled out by the back way, leaving Monty seated on the stool. Moments later, she returned, a fat tentacle of green cactus in her hand. 'Aloe cactus,' she said. 'The Indians say its sap is good for cuts.'

She used the scissors to cut the tentacle lengthwise. It oozed thick sap that looked like green jelly.

'Let me see the wound again,' she said.

Monty tipped his head.

Ann used her forefinger to scrape sap from the aloe and slather it on the scabbed bullet track. 'There,' she said. 'You'll be fine.'

'Thank you, Ann. Feels a lot better.'

'You'd better sit there for a few moments. The aloe will soon dry. Then you can put your hat back on. Would you like to look at shirts while you wait?'

'Ma'am . . . ah . . . Ann. Don't do no good for me to look at shirts. I ain't got no money for to buy them with.'

'Oh, that's all right. You're a cowboy, aren't you? You have a salary, don't you? The US government supports this store so you can pay when you get your salary.' She rummaged behind the counter for a moment and came up with what looked like a hotel registry. 'Make your choice of shirts, sir, and we will record your purchase here with your name and the name of your employer.'

'Well . . . '

'Come.' Ann beckoned him over to some shelves where shirts and trousers and union suits lay folded as if by some careful housewife. She picked a dark maroon shirt. 'I think this would do nicely,' she said, and showed Monty her dazzling smile.

Monty changed in a small closet. When he came out clad in a new union suit, Levi's denim trousers, and the maroon shirt Ann had chosen, he looked and felt like a new man.

'Just write your name and outfit here,' Ann said, setting the open ledger on the counter before him.

He wrote *Monty McCord, Flying W, Watsonville, Colorado*.

'Monty McCord,' Ann said. 'I like that name.'

14

'Boss. Boss.' The Kid hailed Monty as he left the sutler's store with his head full of a woman named Ann.

'Whaddaya want?' Monty's tone said he didn't want to be interrupted.

The Kid slid to a stop. 'Whoa. Didn't mean to get on your wrong side, boss. Just wanted to tell you our cows have showed.'

'Cows're here?'

'Just down the road. Badger Son says they'll be here by noon or so. What're we gonna do?'

'Not much we can do right now. The cows is already bought and paid for. Goldam Barry Seagle got forty thousand bucks for our two thousand critters.'

'We could take it back. The money, I mean.'

'Maybe. What'd the marshal say?'

'Dunno. Sent the wire like you said, though.'

'Then we sit and watch. That's all. Right now, that's all.'

The Kid didn't look satisfied with the situation. Monty wasn't satisfied either, for that matter.

'Tell me, then,' the Kid said.

'Tell you what?'

'Who're you courting, all dressed up like that. Sheesh. Red shirt. Fancy Levi's. Tell ya, boss. You look a little like a tenderfoot.'

'I ain't.'

'I know that. You know that. But no one else does.'

'Got any money?' Monty looked embarrassed to ask.

'Me?'

Monty nodded.

'Dunno. Maybe five bucks'r so.'

Monty held out his hand.

'You want my five bucks?'

'Gimme all you've got,' Monty said.

'Why?'

'I got me an idea. At least a way to

get back some of what's ours.'

'With five bucks?'

'It'll be a start.' Monty still had his hand out.

Reluctantly, the Kid dug crumpled bills from his pocket and handed them over to Monty. 'Damn well better come back to me,' he said.

Monty counted the bills. 'Five bucks, Kid. No mistake.' He shoved the greenbacks into his own pocket. 'I got me a feeling,' he said. 'Barry Seagle's in the Silver Dollar, that rat-eaten place down in hogtown. He's there and I'm gonna get a hunk of our money back from him.'

'Whatcha gonna do?' The Kid had to trot to keep up with Monty as he strode for the hitching rack.

'Play poker.'

'No shit. You think you can outplay Seagle? He's a gambler. That's what he does. You wrangle cows, he wrangles cards. You outta your mind?'

Monty untied Baron's reins from the hitching rail and climbed aboard. He reined the horse around. 'You watch me,' he said, his face set in grim determination. He gigged Baron into a fast trot down the road to hogtown.

Only two horses stood in front of the Silver Dollar when Monty got there. He looped Baron's reins over the rail and plunged into the drinkery.

Three men were belly to the bar. The rest of the Silver Dollar was empty. Monty strode to the bar. 'Where'd Seagle go to?' he said.

'Barry?' the bartender said.

'Yeah. The guy with the poke full of double eagles.'

'He left.'

'I can see that. Where'd he go?'

'How in hell would I know? Someone came in and hollered that a herd was coming. Next thing I knew, the whole place was cleared out. Whiskey?'

'Shit.'

'Whiskey?'

Monty was sorely tempted, but he didn't give in to the urge to have a quick drink. The money in his pocket wasn't his. 'Nah,' he said. 'Reckon I'd better go watch that herd myself.'

The barkeep shrugged. 'Whiskey don't go bad like cider. Come on back when your wolves are kilt.'

Monty raised a hand. 'I'll do'er. If I drink in Uncompahgre, it'll be at the Silver Dollar.' Then he grinned. 'Be obliged if you'd get a bottle or two, though. Maybe some Turley's Mill. Maybe some Old Potrero. That'd be prime.'

The bartender cackled. 'That'll be the day. Once the Utes is outta here, the Army'll leave. Hogtown'll be empty, and I'll be making booze somewhere else. I hear Tombstone's jumping down in Arizona. Maybe I'll go down there.'

'Be proud to know your name, barkeep,' Monty said.

'Me? I don't make no difference nowhere. Name's Clevis. Clevis Banderhaus. Late of Arkansas.'

'Monty McCord. Late of Watsonville by way of El Paso.' Monty headed for the door.

The Kid sat his horse as if he'd been waiting for Monty to make an exit. 'Looks like they'll be holding the herd in Hangtree Meadow,' he said.

Monty untied Baron and mounted. 'We'd better go see what's going on, then.'

'I'm with you, boss,' the Kid said. 'What're we gonna do?'

Monty pulled the Kid's five dollars from his pocket. 'Here. Didn't need this. But thanks anyway.' He handed the bills to the Kid. 'Let's meander over to see our cows.'

'What're we gonna do?'

'Hell, Kid, I don't know. Sometimes all you can do is pray to God some kind of chance comes up.' He headed Baron in the direction of Hangtree Meadow and gave him free rein. He had no idea what to do. Barry Seagle had already been paid for the cows he'd stolen from Ellen Watson. The cows were here in Uncompahgre, five days' drive from their home range. How could they prove the cows were stolen? Knowing

223

sneaky Seagle, he probably had some kind of note that gave him title to 2,000 steers, like the rustlers had for the hundred they drove off H Bar H range. Shit.

Monty heard the cows long before he could see them. He knew by the sound that they were tightly bunched and not allowed to graze freely. Damn. Stupid gunmen'd most likely driven a couple dozen pounds off each steer. Good cowmen take pride in getting a herd to market in good condition. Chico Valdez and his bunch had no such concept. Monty's face clouded up. The Kid followed along behind, saying nothing.

'Damn,' Monty muttered. He pulled Baron up as the thunder of hoofs sounded from back up the trail. He reined the big sorrel off the road and motioned for the Kid to come along. They halted in a copse of jack pines that hid them from casual view.

Moments later, a company of cavalry thundered down the road in a column of twos. The company guidon was in the van, followed by a young lieutenant who leaned to the right so he could hear whatever story Barry Seagle was filling his ear with.

'Goldam Seagle.' Monty swore a string of oaths fit only for muleskinners' ears. He moved Baron back out on the road, eating cavalry dust on the way to Hangtree Meadow. None of the troopers looked back.

'Take it easy, boss. It ain't over yet. Still a long trail back to the Flying W.' The Kid's voice had a hard tone to it. Like he was getting ready for gun play.

'Can't shoot our way out of this one, Kid,' Monty said. The words branded his soul.

⋆ ⋆ ⋆

'Chi-i-ick, chick, chick.' Ellen scattered scraps from the breakfast table across the chicken run. Hens scrambled for the goodies while the wily old rooster stood watch. No chicken hawk or other varmint was going to get his hens while he ruled the roost.

'You watch 'em, old fella,' Ellen said. While the chickens battled for scraps, she checked the coop for eggs. Half a dozen wooden nests lined the back wall. One was occupied, so Ellen left the broody hen alone. From the other nests, she gathered a dozen and a half eggs. Plenty for the short crew at the Flying W with Monty and the boys away. Thinking of Nelson Croft and the life they could build together brought a smile to Ellen Watson's face. And with the H Bar H and the flying W merging, she and Nels would have the largest cow operation in western Colorado. Her smile widened.

Halfway back to the house, her apron heavy with eggs, Ellen heard hoof beats of a running horse, one that had run long and hard. She shaded her eyes to peer eastward toward the dust cloud raised by a single rider headed for Flying W headquarters.

Soon she knew who was coming. Not because her vision was especially sharp, but because she knew how every Flying W cowboy sat his pony. The man racing his three-color paint toward the ranch house was Deerstone.

She quickened her stride to the house, unloaded her egg-laden apron, snatched an old Yellow Boy Winchester from its rack over the kitchen door, checked its load, and went to meet her Ute cowboy.

'What is it?' she said as Deerstone brought the paint to a stiff-legged, hopping stop.

'The herd,' Deerstone said.

'Trouble?'

'Plenty trouble, boss. A bunch of owlhoots, ramrodded by gunman of El Paso name of Chico Valdez, stole our cows.'

Ellen stood speechless.

'They got the cows, boss. Almost all of them.'

For once, Ellen's mind went blank. Everything depended on selling those cattle. Life with Nels. Preserving the Flying W and the H Bar H spreads, building the town her father started. 'Oh my dear God.' It came out more like a prayer than an oath.

Her hand went to her mouth and tears came unbidden to her eyes. 'And,' she managed to say, 'and what happened to Monty McCord?'

'He's gone after the cows,' Deerstone said.

'Alone?'

'With the Kid.' Deerstone dismounted. The paint stood stock still, head down.

'Where are the riders? The drovers?'

'Dead. Hurt. Hurt ones with Uncompahgre Utes.'

'Why are you here, then?'

'Boss, Monty need help, I think.'

'But the herd must be more than halfway to Cheyenne by now. What kind of help could we give Monty? I don't understand.' Ellen, usually the cool-headed person in charge, had trouble grasping the magnitude of the problem. All her mind would say was: *It's all over. Before it even began, it's all over.*

Deerstone brought her back down to earth. 'Cows not going to Cheyenne,' he said. 'Going to Uncompahgre Agency.'

'What? Where?'

'Valdez man turned the cows around. Heads to Uncompahgre Agency, I think.'

'Uncompahgre?'

'Army gets ready to move us Injuns to Uintah Mountains. Need plenty meat for soldiers, a little for Indians.' Deerstone removed his saddle from the three-color and threw it over the corral's top rail. He hung the saddle blanket beside it. 'I ride the buckskin now,' he said. 'OK?'

'Of course. Wait. Ride for H Bar H. Get Nels, er, Nelson Croft and any men he can bring. Meet us at Yellowtail Creek. I'll get Jim and Gerry Swift. We'll ride for Uncompahgre.' Ellen was herself again. Monty and the Kid were following the herd and the rustlers to Uncompahgre Agency. They'd need back-up. The Flying W and H Bar H would provide that help, or die trying. Ellen ran for the house and Deerstone set out to catch the buckskin horse for the ride to the H Bar H, and then on to the Uncompahgre Agency.

'Jim! Jim Blakely!' Ellen hollered.

Blakely answered from the barn.

'Come!' Ellen shouted and punctuated her command with the slamming of the kitchen door. By the time Blakely got to the house, Ellen had shed her Mother Hubbard for a split riding-skirt and denim shirt. She was donning a leather vest when Blakely knocked. 'In!' she called.

'What's up?' Blakely stood just inside the door, hat in hand.

Quickly, Ellen told him about the herd. 'Monty's gonna need back-up,' she said, 'and the brand's got to give it to him. You get Gerry and saddle three horses, and catch three more to give us spare mounts.'

'I'm on it.' Blakely left at a run.

'Sing Chow!'

'Yes, missy,' the Chinese cook called

from the kitchen.

'Trail food for three. Three days' worth. Ready in five minutes.'

'Yes, missy. Ready soon, chop-chop.'

Ellen heard Deerstone's buckskin horse thunder away from the Flying W, going all out.

Nels will come soon. She took comfort in the thought. Jim Blakely and Nelson Croft were probably the most level-headed men in the territory. Not hot-heads like Monty McCord. If only they could beat the herd to Uncompahgre. If only . . .

★　★　★

Chico Valdez rode out from the herd to meet the company of horse soldiers. Monty kept behind the tree line, but he could see well that the Mexican gunman was not pleased with whatever the young lieutenant said to him. Valdez's displeasure affected his horse, which pranced around in a circle, mouthing at its bit.

The lieutenant barked an order and the troops split off to surround the herd and relieve the men who were holding it there in Hangtree Meadow. The gunmen-drovers gathered around Chico, the lieutenant, and Barry Seagle. Barry handed each man some money. Monty caught the glint of gold coins and reckoned this was payoff.

The gunmen-drovers whooped and hollered, and as a man, gigged their tired ponies into a lope. They streamed past Monty and the Kid, headed for hogtown, the only place they could wet their whistles after the long dry ride.

'Wonder what got Valdez so upset?' Monty said, keeping his voice low.

The Kid shrugged.

Valdez threw up his hands in exasperation, turned his horse, and set out after the other gunmen. He ignored Monty and the Kid, but Monty was sure he knew they were there.

'I reckon the whole hornet's nest is gonna end up in the Silver Dollar,' Monty said. 'That might be the place to do whatever it is we're gonna do.'

'What are we gonna do?' the Kid said.

'Wish I knew,' Monty said. 'Wish I knew.'

Barry Seagle and the lieutenant rode back along the road, Seagle again in deep conversation with the young officer. Neither noticed the two horsemen back in the trees.

When Seagle and the lieutenant were out of sight, Monty reined Baron back on to the road. He spoke to the Kid. 'Might do you good to visit your blood brother for a day or two,' he said.

'Won't,' the Kid said. 'I ride for the Flying W and you're the trail boss. I'll be sticking with you come hell or high water.' The Kid's face was grave. Monty could see he'd made up his mind.

'OK, Kid,' he said. 'It's your ass.'

'It is that.'

Monty gigged Baron back onto the road and pointed him toward Fort Uncompahgre's hogtown. He didn't relish trading shots with Chico Valdez, especially without his Colt. He touched the stock of the old Sharps that occupied the boot where his '73 Winchester had been. *Shee-it. Army's got the beeves. Seagle's got the money. Marshal Slade ain't showed up. Me and the Kid's gotta go it alone. Double shee-it.*

Baron used his gentle single-foot pace to eat up the distance to hogtown. The Kid kept his horse's head at Monty's stirrup, and when they reached the first ramshackle dwellings, he instinctively drew his Colt, twirled the cylinder, checked the action, fed a sixth bullet into it, and shoved the gun back into the holster at his side.

'Gunning for someone?' Monty asked.

'You taught me to be ready for anything that comes down the pike, boss.'

'Yeah, 'n' me without no hogleg or even a good lever-action Winchester.'

'You got all them new duds, how come you never got no six-gun?'

Monty almost stopped his horse. 'I

never thought of it,' he said. 'I'll do it now.'

Baron's single-foot was as fast as a horse could go without breaking into a lope, so Monty just sat, watching the shacks drift by, sometimes with women out doing their household chores, sometimes with small children playing with sticks and stones. *What was that little song? Sticks and stones may break my bones but names can never hurt me?* Like hell.

'I'll go keep my eye on 'em,' the Kid said, nodding at the horses tied out front of the Silver Dollar. They included the big black that Valdez rode and Seagle's tall skinny bay.

The Kid reined his horse over to a stunted scrub oak. 'I'll be here,' he said.

Baron single-footed on to the sutler's store with Monty aboard.

'Why Mr McCord. How nice to see you again.' Ann's contralto voice raised goose-bumps all up and down Monty's spine. No woman had ever done that before, but the feeling was not altogether unpleasant.

'Is there some way I can be of further assistance, sir?' she said.

Monty still hadn't found his tongue. He snatched his hat from his head and stood there like the dumbstruck cowboy he was.

'Well, sir?' she said.

'I gotta have a gun,' he said.

15

Monty McCord never thought of himself as a gunhand. To him, a six-gun was a tool, no more and no less than a lariat or a running iron or a good Texas saddle. A man had to practise with a tool a lot to use it well. He couldn't sit a saddle well unless he'd spent countless hours riding the line or rounding up in the spring to count and brand the calf crop.

He walked out of the Uncompahgre Agency sutler's store with a M1875 Remington Army .45 shoved behind the waistband of his Levi's and Ann's image burned forever on his heart. Once this flap over stolen cows was over, Monty McCord would come calling at the sutler's store. He surely would.

Baron waited patiently, as was his wont, but he'd clearly cropped off every green shoot within reach. 'Back to the Silver Dollar,' Monty said as he mounted the big sorrel. 'Let's just see where this row is gonna take us.'

Noise from the Silver Dollar reached Monty even before the rawhide saloon was in sight. He pulled the Remington out and checked its loads. Six .45 bullets. Straight from the box of fifty rounds in his offside pocket. The action operated with smooth efficiency. The soft smell of gun oil wafted. He replaced the Remington and stopped Baron on the far side of the Kid's pony. He tied Baron's reins to the same scrub oak.

The Silver Dollar's front door stood wide open. The crowd of men, and now women, seethed like maggots in an open wound. Men with money were in hogtown and every Army hanger-on was at the Silver Dollar, looking to relieve those men of their fortune, hard-earned or not.

No one paid Monty the slightest attention as he pushed his way through the seething bodies to the bar. Clevis wandered over to him.

'Ain't got much money, Clevis,' Monty said. 'Maybe enough for a beer.'

Clevis tipped his head back and laughed. 'Monty. This here's a one-drink outfit. You drink whiskey, or you don't drink.'

'But I ain't got but one thin dime.'

Clevis grabbed a cloudy glass from the shelf behind the bar. He sloped off to the whiskey barrel and dippered the glass half-full. Back in front of Monty, he plonked the glass down on the bar. 'Dime,' he said.

Monty dug in the pocket of his new Levi's and found the dime. 'Here.' He pushed it across the bar.

Clevis grinned. 'Thankee.'

The half-full glass of rotgut in hand, Monty turned and hooked his elbows on the edge of the bar. He surveyed the Silver Dollar's roiling crowd.

The tables were full of gunmen-drovers, women, and hangers-on. The saloon was crowded all right, but that

239

didn't mean a lot of people. Monty's greasy old Stetson sat low over his eyes. With his new shirt and Levi's, he looked a lot different from before. With luck, no one would recognize him. Valdez had only seen him from a distance, and the hired gunmen-drovers knew him not at all. The only person who might recognize him was Barry Seagle, who was deep in a card game with the house shark and Chico Valdez. Monty gradually moved down the bar until he was at the back wall. He'd left the old Sharps in the saddle boot, so he wasn't burdened by it. He touched the butt of the Remington Army as if to be reassured that it was there, ready for action.

Although the Silver Dollar was full of rowdy voices, the three men at the back table sat silent. Each knew the cards and concentrated solely on the game. In fact, nothing about the card players was unusual, except the pile of gold coins in front of the players and in the middle of the table.

A gaggle of drinkers and women gathered around the table. 'These'ns is playing eagle ante,' a man with a graying spade-beard hollered. 'Looket that moola. Buy me a whole barrel a red-eye with that, and a month of pokes with Janey Sue.' He brayed like a jackass at his own jest.

More people gathered round the game table. The chance of Seagle noticing Monty decreased as the watchers increased. He was there. Seagle was there. Valdez was there. But Monty couldn't think of anything to do. He sipped at the whiskey.

'Didn't expect to see you around,' Clevis said. He'd moved down the bar and leaned over to put his mouth closer to Monty's ear.

'Me neither. But a man has to ride for his brand.'

'Yeah. So what?'

'Them cows what come, they wear Flying W brands. My brand.'

'No shit.'

Monty nodded, never taking his eyes

off the game table. The house shark played casually, his eyes mere slits as he watched the game unfold. Seagle sat with his back to the far wall, turned slightly away from Monty, but the smirk on his face was clearly visible. It was a three-hand game, but Monty could tell that Valdez played against Seagle alone, ignoring the house gambler.

Monty sipped the rotgut booze. The day dragged on. The crowd ebbed and flowed, sometimes bolstered by off-duty soldiers, sometimes reduced when time came to eat — or sleep, as the case might be. Some of the sleeping, of course, took place in the cribs of the dirty doves that seemed to come out of the gutters when the number of drinking males in the Silver Dollar increased.

Monty stood and stood, wetting his lips once in a while with the glass of Clevis's home-made whiskey. The level of liquid in the glass never did reduce by much, but no one in the saloon paid attention to how other folks were drinking.

The piles of gold coins in front of the gamblers also ebbed and flowed, now piling up in front of the house gambler, now in front of Valdez, now in front of Seagle, but a few more eagles stuck to Seagle's pile than to Valdez's. A smoky, angry look began to inhabit the Mexican gunman's face.

Seagle became the dealer, and the pile of coins in front of him took a sudden jump. Valdez didn't like it, or so the scowl on his face said.

'New cards,' Seagle hollered.

'Play with what you've got,' Clevis answered. 'This ain't no Fancy Dan Cheyenne Social Club.'

Sour-faced, Seagle shuffled the deck and began the deal. Monty watched him closely, and still he almost missed the way he stacked the deck. Seagle was even cleverer than most house players, but greed seemed to have gotten the best of him. His eyes glowed every time he looked at the stack of eagles and double eagles near his left hand. Maybe he wanted to force Valdez into doing something. Maybe he just wanted all the coin on the table. Maybe he just didn't care. At any rate, Seagle stacked the deck.

At last, Valdez pushed all the coins he had into the center of the table. He had just enough to call, but Valdez's two pair were no match for Seagle's full house. He jumped to his feet. '*¡Tramposo!* You cheat.'

'Don't be a bad loser, Chico,' Seagle said, a smile on his face. 'The luck is in the cards.'

Valdez leaned over the table. 'I — say — you — cheat. Gutless buzzard.'

The smile dropped from Seagle's face. 'Luck,' he said. 'Purest luck. No more. No less.'

'I say you lie, *gringo glotón*.'

'It's time for me to go,' Seagle said, raking the pot over to his side of the table. 'Gentlemen, thank you for the pleasant game.'

'You are a liar and a cheat, Barry

Seagle, a liar and a cheat.' Valdez turned on his heel and took two steps toward the bar. Seagle pulled a derringer from his pocket, cocking it as it came.

Valdez took a sudden big step to the right as the click of the cocking weapon reached his ears. He crouched and drew his own Colt as the sharp cough of the derringer spat lead in his direction. The little bullet plucked at the loose fabric of Valdez's shirt. 'If you shoot, don't miss,' he said, and pulled the Colt's trigger.

Valdez's bullet took Seagle low in the throat. He fell over backward, clawing at the bloody hole below his larynx. His head thudded against the wall, and he crumpled to the floor. His heels beat out a dying tattoo.

'Luck of the draw,' Valdez said, the smoking Colt still in his hand. The quiet in the Silver Dollar was like everyone was holding their breath. Valdez stepped back to the table, removed his hat, and placed it upside down on a chair. His Colt held ready in his hand, he moved the chair under the edge of the table and scraped Seagle's hoard of gold into the hat. Then, hat in one hand and Colt in the other, Valdez made his way to the door. Monty followed. *Where's the Kid?*

Outside, the Mexican gunman strode to his horse, a big black with one white foreleg and a white blaze on its face. He opened the flap of the onside saddle-bag and dumped in the hatful of gold coins.

Monty stood for a moment in the doorway of the Silver Dollar. Chico Valdez checked his saddle cinch as if he were in no hurry. As he raised his left foot toward the stirrup, a voice stopped him.

'Chico Valdez!' The Kid stepped away from the scrub oak and out into the road that cut through the middle of hogtown.

Valdez had both hands on his saddle, a difficult position to be in when another gunman calls, although Monty never thought of the Kid as a gunman.

'What do you want, *muchacho*?' Valdez put his foot back down and turned to face the Kid.

'Three years ago, you gunned down Elfred Denton,' the Kid said.

'So?'

'Elfred Denton was my mother's onliest brother.'

Valdez straightened. 'So?'

'My pa's dead. My uncle had no kids.'

Valdez shrugged and settled himself, feet shoulder-width apart, hands hanging naturally. 'If you have some quarrel with me, *muchacho*, I am ready. I do not remember killing this Denton man, but I do not ask the name of men before I kill them. Perhaps I should. What is your name, *muchacho*, that I may know who I kill?'

The Kid stood a little straighter, fully five six, maybe five seven, in his stockinged feet. A few black whiskers were beginning to show on his upper lip. 'I'm Elroy Daws. Most people called my pa Sudden. They call me Kid.

247

You've killed too many, Valdez. Now it's your turn to die.'

'*Muchacho*. You think you can kill Chico Valdez? Do you want everyone here to howl with laughter as you die? Take my advice, *muchacho*. Walk away. I have killed one man today and that is enough. Perhaps.' As he spoke, Valdez made his move. His right hand plucked the Colt at his side from its holster, cocking the hammer with the web of the thumb as he drew. Valdez was quick, and the kind of man who never drew but to kill. Still, his gun had barely come level when the Kid's first bullet took Valdez just below the collarbone on his left side. Valdez staggered, then steadied, and tried to raise his pistol again. The Kid's second shot caught him just below the breastbone, making him take a step back. He tried to lift the big Colt, tried to line up its five-and-a-half-inch barrel with the Kid, tried to get off one deadly shot, tried . . .

The thunder of horse's hoofs came from the road to Hangtree Meadow.

The Kid paid the noise no mind. He watched Valdez like a hawk watches a field mouse.

The Mexican gunman fell to his knees. '*Muchacho. Muchacho*,' he said, as if it took great effort to build the words. He fired the Colt into the dust of the street three feet in front of him, then toppled sideways. Blood gushed from his open mouth. His last breath stirred a small puff of dust.

The Kid didn't move.

'It's done, Kid,' Monty said.

A group of riders pounded up the road, Jim Blakely in the lead with Nelson Croft and Ellen Watson just behind him.

The Kid holstered his six-gun, went to Valdez's big black horse, unstrapped the saddle-bags from behind the cantle, and put them over his shoulder. He moved over to stand beside Monty McCord.

When the shooting stopped, men and doves poured out of the Silver Dollar.

Flying W and H Bar H cowhands

rode up with Winchesters across their saddlebows. 'Gentlemen,' Jim Blakely said, 'we'd take it as a friendly gesture if you'd all use your thumb and finger to take out your hardware and drop 'em on the ground.'

The drinkers complied.

'Thank you, gentlemen,' Blakely said. 'Monty? Who ought we to hold here?'

'Valdez shot Seagle dead. The Kid shot Valdez dead. That's about it.'

'Who rustled our cows?'

'Seagle, 'n' Valdez was ramrodding it, I reckon.'

Blakely turned in his saddle. 'Boss,' he said to Ellen, 'likely this goes farther than we figure. Ain't likely the Army would buy stock without seeing a bill of sale.'

The Kid spoke up. 'I sent for Marshal Slade, but don't know if he's coming.'

Ellen snicked at her horse and he moved up even with Blakely. The Kid held out the saddle-bags. Ellen's eyebrows rose in a question.

'This here's all the gold coins that Valdez and Seagle and the house shark was gambling over. I reckon they're yours.'

'You did good, Kid.' Blakely reached down for the saddle-bag. 'Damn. Some heavy. More'n a couple thousand dollars in this, boss.'

'I reckon,' said the Kid, 'but it ain't all. Not by a long shot.'

Monty decided to let somebody else worry about the money. His thoughts were on Cinch, dead across the fire, Gabe Baca, a lump of cold flesh, Heck Lewis, shot in the back, and the other cowpokes wounded and stove up. He walked through the Silver Dollar drinkers. He brought up the sight of men crowing over gold coins at Hangtree Meadow.

'Boss,' he said, 'some of these dumb-asses were in on killing Flying W and H Bar H waddies. I seen them with the herd. What say we hold them and let the hogtown people go?'

'Do it,' Blakely said.

Monty walked to his horse with measured steps. He pulled the old Sharps from the boot, checked its load, eared the hammer back, and marched toward the gaggle of people in front of the Silver Dollar.

'Kid, come 'ere.'

'Whacha need, boss?'

'You keep 'em covered.'

The Kid drew his Remington.

One by one, Monty fingered the hired guns who'd been with Valdez and the herd at Hangtree Meadow.

16

With Jim Blakely, Nels Croft, and the Flying W and H Bar H riders holding loaded and cocked Winchesters, the gang brought by Valdez and paid by Seagle could do nothing but stand there, their hardware in the dust beside them. All at once, Monty found himself with nothing to do. A squad of horsesoldiers arrived in a cloud of dust, led by a spit-shine major. US Marshal Cameron Slade rode beside the officer. Monty sidled over to stand by Baron, where he hoped he'd go unnoticed by the lawman.

Cameron tipped his hat to Ellen Watson. 'Ma'am,' he said. 'Got a wire from Monty McCord that said your herd'd been rustled. That true?'

Monty said nothing.

'That's right, Marshal,' Ellen said. 'The man who stood behind the plot is

253

dead. He lies inside the Silver Dollar. The man he brought to do the deed lies dead over there.' She pointed at Chico Valdez's corpse.

'I recognize Valdez,' Slade said. 'Who's in the saloon?'

'Barry Seagle.'

'And who are these men you've got under the gun?'

'The owlhoots Valdez hired to steal our herd,' Ellen said. 'Good cowboys are dead, Marshal, because of these men.'

Slade turned to the major. 'Can we borrow your guard-house, Major?'

The major gave a curt nod.

'Excellent. Then, if your men could escort these . . . rustlers to the fort, I'll stay a moment and see that the dead are properly cared for.'

'Of course,' the major said. 'You heard the marshal, Sergeant. Escort these outlaws to the guardhouse. You can release Ericson to make room.'

The sergeant gave the major a brisk salute and barked at the gunmen. 'You.

Line up by twos. Now. March!'

The rustlers straggled off toward Fort Uncompahgre with the squad of cavalrymen keeping them on the straight and narrow.

'Monty McCord.'

Monty started. He'd figured it was all over as far as he was concerned. 'Yeah. Right here, Marshal.'

'Come with me,' Slade said. 'Let's go see what's inside.'

'Me?'

'Yes, you. You're a material witness, you know. Come on.'

'OK, Marshal. I'm coming.' Monty followed Slade into the gloomy innards of the Silver Dollar. The Kid stayed with the horses by the scrub oak.

Seagle's body and Clevis were the only occupants of the Silver Dollar.

'Goldam you, Monty McCord,' Clevis said. 'You all scared away my drinking people.' He noticed the star-in-shield badge on Slade's vest. 'An' a goldam lawman, too. Shee-it.'

'How much for a drink?' Slade said.

'Dollar. Cash.'

Slade put a double eagle on the bar. 'Give us enough time to drink that much, man. Then we'll be outta here.'

'You got it.' The gold coin put a smile back on Clevis's face. 'Good friends, you got, Monty,' he said.

Monty couldn't resist. 'Ol' drinking buddy,' he said.

Slade shot him a stern glance. 'Let's have a look at Seagle.' He squatted by the body.

Seagle's eyes were still wide open and his mouth formed a silent scream.

Slade scowled. 'Come help, Monty. Get over there on his other side.'

Monty did as he was told, and squatted down by Seagle across from Slade. The marshal started going through the gambler's pockets. The vest pockets held only a watch. From the inside pocket of Seagle's coat he withdrew a leather wallet. He unfolded it and shook its contents out on the table — some folding money, some papers, and a small key.

Slade found a few coins in the pants pocket, along with four .41 caliber bullets. 'That's it,' he said. 'Let's see what's so important about those papers.' He picked one up and unfolded it.

'Well, well, well.'

'Whatcha got, Marshal?' Monty strained to see what was written on the paper.

Slade held the paper up. 'This says Wells Fargo will pay the bearer twenty thousand dollars in gold.' The marshal folded the paper. 'Wonder why?'

'Flying W and H Bar H cows,' Monty said. 'I reckon that'd be about half the going price on a government place like this.'

'Major Higgins said the Army hadn't paid for the stock,' Slade said.

'That leaves the Indian Agent, then.'

'It does at that.' The marshal squatted back down by the corpse. 'Those saddle-bags full of double eagles. That's probably not more than a couple of thousand, maybe a little more.' Slade checked shirt pockets. The dead man's gut rumbled. Gas was building up already. Slade ran his hand down the front of the blood-splattered vest. His hand stopped just above Seagle's waist. 'Well, well, well. Our gambler doesn't leave much to chance,' he said. He unbuttoned the vest, then the shirt, and pulled the shirt's tail from the trousers. The canvas money belt around Seagle's waist gave off dull clinks.

'Shee-it,' Monty said.

'I reckon it's gold coins,' Slade said. 'Likely double eagles.'

The marshal unbuckled the money belt and pulled it from Seagle's stiffening body. He grunted softly as he lifted the heavy belt. 'Ten pockets,' he said. He put the belt on the table. Again, dull clinks. Each bulging pocket held twenty double eagles. 'Four thousand more dollars,' Slade said, as if he were talking to himself. 'What's the going price for beeves?'

'Might get twenty-three dollars a head in Cheyenne,' Monty said.

'What here?'

'Dunno. Maybe twenty.'

'So we're talking of something in the neighborhood of forty thousand bucks.'

'I said that a minute ago.'

'Don't get sassy. You still gotta stand trial for shooting that Billings kid.' Slade studied the corpse. 'Where'd you put the money, old son?' he asked. Seagle didn't answer.

'Maybe we'd better find out how much Seagle was really paid,' Monty said. 'Army says it didn't, right? So that leaves the goldam Indian Agent.'

Slade called to the barman. 'Say? Will that double eagle take care of getting this corpse buried?'

Clevis scowled. 'I reckon,' he said. 'Can't just let it lay there and rot. Bad for business.'

'Good, and thank you.' Slade put the papers back in the wallet and shoved it into his own pocket. 'Let's go, Monty.'

Uncompahgre Indian Agent Carl Riess put his quill pen back in its holder and leaned back in his chair as Marshal Cameron Slade and Monty McCord strode into his office.

'Gentlemen, how can I help you?'

'The Army tells me you bought a herd of beef,' Slade said.

'That I did. That I did. Two thousand steers. Gotta feed those hungry soldiers. Oh, and the Uncompahgre Utes, too, you know.'

Monty McCord's face got granite-hard. The muscles along his jaw bunched as he ground his teeth. 'You dirty son of a bitch. You paid that asshole Barry Seagle for cows wearing my brand.'

'*Your* brand?'

'*My* brand. I ride for the Flying W. I was trail boss for that herd that Chico Valdez stole. Him and his gunnies shot me.' Monty whipped off his hat. The groove the bullet had carved in his scalp stood out, the hair around cut short by Ann over at the sutler's. 'Pure luck that I ain't dead by a rustler's bullet. Dead like Cinch McDougal. Dead like Gabe Baca. Dead like Heck Willis. Dead for the money you paid Barry Seagle.'

Monty leaned across the desk, took a handful of Riess's shirt and jerked him upright. 'Scum.'

'Unhand me,' Riess squeaked.

'Monty.'

Monty reared back with his fist cocked.

'Monty!' Slade said again. 'Smacking a government man won't help.'

Fist still cocked, Monty shot a glance at Slade. He heaved a sigh, then let Riess drop back into his chair. 'You figure it out, Marshal. I'll wait outside.'

Fuming, Monty went outside the agency building, just to keep himself from breaking back into the agent's office and beating the shit out of him. He leaned against the wall in the sunshine; after a bit he dug into his pocket for the makings and realized he didn't have any. A reason to go to the sutler's store across the way. A reason to see if Ann . . . what was her last name . . . ? was there. Bull Durham, that's what he needed, and some papers and some lucifers. And while he strolled

261

over to the sutler's, his irritation evaporated.

A little bell tinkled when Monty opened the sutler store's door, and Ann came into the store from the back rooms, wiping her hands on her apron. Her smile got bigger and bigger.

'Why Mr McCord. It's so good to see you again so soon.'

'Yes, well, me and Marshal Slade, US Marshal Slade, that is, me and the marshal were clearing up a little something with the Indian Agent.'

'Uncle Carl?'

Monty stopped dead. 'Uncle Carl?'

'Carl Riess, the Indian Agent. He's my uncle. That's why I'm here.' Ann's sweet face grew sad and tears threatened to flood over the long lashes of her lower eyelids. 'After my folks died of cholera, Uncle Carl's the only relative I have. He was good enough to give me the responsibility of looking after customers here in the store.'

'I owe money to that . . . ' Monty couldn't think of an epithet that he could say in front of a lady like Ann, so he let it slide.

Ann looked perplexed. 'Why are you upset at having a tab — that's what they call it, isn't it — a tab here at the store?'

'Ann. Listen to me. That . . . your Uncle Carl bought two thousand beeves that was rustled from my brand, from the Flying W. And I'm thinking he had a deal with that gambler Barry Seagle before we even started the drive.' Monty paused as a new thought hit him. 'I wonder how much Carl Riess made off that deal,' he said. 'I wonder.'

Monty about-faced to head out through the door. 'I'll be back, Ann, I surely will.' He went back to the agency at a trot, and burst through the door like a four-year-old.

'Marshal. Marshal.'

Slade looked up from his seat in front of Riess's desk, his eyebrows raised at Monty's clatter.

Riess cringed as Monty leaned over his desk again, both hands palm down on the top.

'Marshal, I've been talking to Ann over to the sutler's. She's this shit-for-brains asshole's niece. What she said got me wondering as to how much this here agent got for buying beeves he knew was stole.'

Riess stared straight ahead, ignoring Monty.

'What about that, Riess?' Cameron Slade's voice was rock hard.

Riess cleared his throat. 'Marshal, I assure you, I only bought cattle that I was assured were free and clear.'

'Proof?'

Riess opened the middle drawer of his desk and extracted a sheet of paper. 'Here.' He shoved it across the desk.

Slade looked at it. 'Receipt from Barry Seagle, eh? Forty thousand. Any of that gold rub off on your hands, Riess?'

Riess puffed up. 'Sir? Certainly not. What do you take me for? A thief?'

'I've yet to meet an Indian Agent that wasn't,' Slade said, 'but I can't prove it. Right now, I can't.'

Riess smiled and relaxed. 'I'd think not, as I did nothing wrong.'

'Shee-it,' Monty said. 'Give me five minutes along with this asshole, Marshal, just me and Badger Son, that young Ute. He's outside somewhere. Give us five minutes. He'll talk.'

'Marshal, are you going to let a mere cowboy talk like that to an agent of the Government of the United States?'

'Free country, Riess, and I don't hear no libel outta Monty.'

Monty pulled the leather gloves from behind his belt and carefully pulled them on, flexing the fingers and making fists.

'Leave it be, Monty. Leave it be for now.' Slade stood. 'Let's go,' he said.

Monty didn't like it, but he left, with Carl Riess sitting there at his desk with a shit-eating grin on his face.

★   ★   ★

'OK, Ellen,' Slade said. 'This is the best we can do right now.' He handed her the Wells Fargo draft and Seagle's money belt. 'You've got the saddle-bags from Valdez, and the little that was in his pockets. Ain't near enough, but maybe it's a hell of a lot better than nothing.'

Ellen nodded. 'Much, much better than nothing, Marshal. Very much.'

'One more thing, El.' Slade pulled out the leather wallet he'd found on Seagle's body. 'You'll be wanting this. The gambler won't need it any more.'

With questions in her eyes, Ellen opened the wallet. A few greenbacks on one side, several papers on the other. She extracted a paper and opened it. 'Wha-a-a-t? Cam. This is the eight-thousand-dollar Billing note.'

'Look at the others.'

'Notes. Notes. Four, no, five of them.' Ellen looked up, her eyes again brimming. 'So many people in Watson-ville will be so glad to tear these up. Thank you, Cameron Slade.'

Slade touched his hat with a finger. A tiny smile played at the corner of his mouth. 'If that's all, El, I'll be going over to the fort to have a talk with the prisoners. I'll come over to Watsonville when things are straightened out.'

Monty cleared his throat. 'Boss?'

Ellen gave him a glance as she was digging in the saddle-bags.

'I'm outta fixings, boss. I'd like to jog over to the sutler's and git some afore we ride for the Flying W.'

'Here, Monty.' She held out a small leather poke. 'Five hundred of this is yours, and there's a hundred for each man on the drive. You give the men their wages.'

'Me?'

'You're the trail boss. You take care of the men.'

Monty's smile threatened to break his jaw. 'I'll do it, boss. You know I will.' He took the poke and gigged Baron toward the agency. 'Be back shortly. If you've ridden for home, I'll ketch up.'

Ellen nodded to Jim Blakely. 'Line out,' he said. 'We're going home.'

Monty McCord came back from the sutler's store completely satisfied. He had Bull Durham, papers, lucifers, and Ann's permission for him to visit. Humming just came naturally as he moved through Hangtree Meadow, but he didn't sing. Baron would have objected to that. On the far side of the meadow, just before dropping down to follow the Uncompahgre River, Monty felt he was being followed. He shucked the old Sharps from the saddle boot and stopped Baron just past the tree line in a copse of jack pines. He held the Sharps across his saddlebows and watched his back trail. There she came. A thousand pounds of brindle cow, horns seven feet if an inch, bound and determined to follow Monty McCord, wherever he would go.

Monty nudged Baron out to the trail. 'Come on, Brindle. Come on,' he echoed Jim Blakely. 'We're going home.'

Epilogue

On the sly, Ellen Watson returned the notes Seagle had held on people in Watsonville. Monty McCord rode hard for Uncompahgre Agency every time he had a couple of days free. Then Marshal Cameron Slade came riding up to the Flying W headquarters.

'Cam, how are you?' Ellen said from the front door. 'Long ride on a Sunday. What can we do for you?'

'Serious matter, Ellen. Serious.'

She didn't catch the little twinkle in his eye. 'Oh my. Gracious. Well, come in. Let me hear whatever it is.'

'Got coffee on?'

'We always have coffee on, you know that.'

'We'd better have some then, because Nels and Jim and Monty McCord should be here, so I don't have to explain things twice.'

'Nels is at the H Bar H. Mr Billings is doing poorly. But Jim and Monty should be around.'

'Then you'll have to tell Nels.'

'I can do that. Let me send for Jim and Monty. And get you coffee.' She brought cup and saucer from the kitchen with a two-quart coffee pot. 'Black?'

Slade nodded. He sipped at the coffee, relishing the aroma and bitter taste, running the situation over in his mind. Ellen came back in with Jim and Monty before he could even finish the first cup.

Jim and Monty dragged out chairs and sat down, Ellen went for more coffee. The lack of conversation was deafening.

'So what is it, Cameron?' Ellen said as she sat down with her own cup of steaming brew.

'Well. I'll make a long story very short. Carl Riess was cheating the government big scale.' He tossed a canvas poke into the middle of the table. 'There's the kickback Seagle paid him to take your herd. Two thousand dollars. But he's been selling goods that were supposed to be distributed to the Utes and pocketing the money. Like you've probably heard, the agency is closing, and the Uncompahgre's will be moved to Uintah Basin.'

Slade brought a roll of bills from his hip pocket and put them in front of Monty. 'Barry Seagle was wanted in three states for everything from con games to murder. That's your reward money.'

'Mine? I never done nothing.'

'You kept after the herd, even when you was shot. Enough by my book.'

'What about the Kid?'

Slade tossed a small poke on the table. 'Five hundred on Chico Valdez, dead or alive. I reckon that's the Kid's.'

Monty gulped. 'I reckon.' He turned to Ellen. 'Boss?'

She smiled. 'It's yours, Monty. All yours.'

'Shee-it. Oh, sorry boss.' Monty

picked up the roll of bills. He smoothed the greenbacks out. Hundreds. Fifties. Twenties. Slightly over fifteen hundred in all. He looked at Ellen for confirmation. She nodded.

'Hot damn!' It was hard for Monty to think straight for a while, and before he really came back to earth, Cameron Slade left. Jim went outside. Ellen got the coffee pot from the kitchen and freshened Monty's cup. 'I heard about the Rafter 7, Monty. You gave Ben Stacey three hundred down-payment for that rat trap. That's what I hear.'

Monty turned the cup around in the saucer by its handle. He didn't look at Ellen. 'Yeah. He was just gonna leave. I figured he could use the money. He said three hundred was more'n he expected, and he gave me a bill of sale for the place. I reckon it's mine.'

'You're quitting me?'

'No, boss. Well, not right away. Well, I thought maybe I could stay on at the Flying W. Maybe buy some calves from you in the spring. Build my herd real slow while running it with the Flying W stuff. I was hoping . . . '

Ellen gave Monty a bright smile. 'Monty McCord, without you, there might not even be any Flying W or H Bar H. You're more than welcome to work here and fix up the Rafter 7 when you have extra time.'

'Um, it ain't the Rafter 7 any more, boss. We'll call it the MA Connected, Ann and me. The MA Connected. Oh, and I'd like to buy that old brindle cow.'

THE END

Other titles in the
Linford Western Library:

THE DEVIL'S WORK

Paul Bedford

Marshal Rance Toller is locking up a pair of troublemakers when Angie Sutter, a homesteader from a nearby valley, arrives with the news that her husband was murdered that morning. Whilst Rance has qualms about heading out into the frozen wasteland, leaving only an ageing deputy to stand guard, he accompanies Angie to her cabin — to find not only Jacob Sutter's body, but also that of his neighbour, slain by the same weapon. Meanwhile, back at the jailhouse, the deputy is dead and the prisoners gone . . .

REBEL RAIDERS

John Dyson

A gang of former Confederate soldiers is robbing and killing its way across Kansas. Novice lawman Cass Clacy is sent out after them, but what chance does he have of outgunning such experienced fighters? When Sheriff Jim Clarke joins Cass in the chase, his main aim is a share of the reward. Together they penetrate deep into the heart of the Indian Nations, where Cass falls under the spell of the lovely Audrey — but can he save her from the clutches of the dangerous Josiah Baines?

THE COMANCHE FIGHTS AGAIN

D. M. Harrison

Mitch Bayfield, known as 'Broke', was kidnapped and raised as a Comanche. When, many years later, he looks for his kin, he finds himself unable to settle in either world and turns his back on them all. He is determined, however, to return and liberate Little Bluestem, another white captive. The two of them flee, with the Comanche hot on their trail — but they are about to tangle with a ruthless gang of bank robbers . . .

THE PRISONER OF GUN HILL

Owen G. Irons

When Luke Walsh falls for the beautiful Dee Dee Bright, he makes the biggest mistake of his young life. After she tricks him into killing the marshal of Tucson, Arizona, there is nothing for it but to take to the desert. But when his horse founders, he finds himself afoot and alone on the plain. Picked up by a passing wagon, he is set to work as slave labour in the Gun Hill gold mine — the remote outpost harbouring a nest of dangerous outlaws . . .

CLIMAX

C. J. Sommers

There isn't much to the town of Climax: just another dusty, wind-blown community biding its time until the desert reclaims it. Then its council decides that maintaining a marshal is an unnecessary expenditure. With the town having dispensed with his services, ex-Marshal Frost is let go to make his way out onto the desert — but that is the signal the gathering outlaw gang has been waiting for. They want Climax, and mean to make it their hideout: an outlaw town where they rule the roost . . .

TO KILL THE VALKO KID

Michael D. George

Retired marshal Clem Everett rides into Sioux City moments after the infamous Johnny Sunset arrives. It's not long before Clem discovers that Sunset is there to claim the reward money on the lawman's old pal Valko. From an arrangement made way back, Clem knows Valko is due to appear in the city the next day. The clock is ticking towards midnight, and there is no way to warn his friend that the deadliest bounty hunter in the West is intent on gunning him down . . .